"The Love Of Many, Shall Wax Cold"

A Novel By Warren Dean

"The Love of Many Shall Wax Cold"

Warren Dean

The Gateway
Chapter 1

In the high mountains of central Utah, an old man loads his tools in his truck after a days work at his cabin. It's near midnight as he drives through the aspen trees toward the gate. His long time companion, Doggers Lu, a Beagle in the back seat is agitated and alert, she peers out of the truck windows into the darkness. The old man flipped on his new LED lights as he drove through the thick wooded forest toward the gate. "Look at that Doggers, they light up the whole night." Said the old man. He put the truck in park and told the dog, "now don't lock me out!" He climbed out of the cab and walked toward the locked gate, fumbling with the chain, his hands rough and callused, swollen with arthritis, pulling the gate open, he stepped back in his truck to drive it through the opening in the aspen log stacked fence. As he steps back out to close and lock the gate, his Beagle growls deeply. He turns and says, "what is it Doggers?" She growls intensely while starring out of the back window. The old man looks at her, the hair is standing up on her neck, he turns and stares out into the dark forest. He sees nothing, but a wave of fear runs through him. He pauses for a moment then quietly says, "Bullshit" calming his own fear. He walks into the darkness behind the truck, as he pulls the gate closed he hears his dog begin to scream and howl as if in a dog fight. He stops and turns to the right, peering out into the darkness, he sees nothing, but senses something, his primal instincts on high alert, adrenaline pumps through him, his old heart begins to race, he knows something is there but what? He takes a deep breath and steps toward his truck. His mind and body compelling him to run as never before, his hands and arms begin to shake, yet he controls himself, he walks deliberately, his pride refusing to give into fear. Out of his peripheral vision, he sees it, a huge dark movement which is suddenly upon him with great violence, his last emotion, absolute terror, and then he is gone. His Beagle companion screaming and howling inside the truck, frantically chewing and clawing at the interior trying to get out and defend her man.

8:45AM the next morning, a minivan passes the still idling truck parked near the side of the dirt road, steam coming off the trucks exhaust in the crisp morning air. A mother is taking her daughter to girls camp, some two miles further on the road. She passes by the truck and notices a dog starring blankly out of the back window.   After two hours of introductions and orientation at the girls camp, the mother says her goodbyes to her daughter with a promise to return in one weeks time. As she drives back she approaches the parked truck, she sees another mini van parked next to it with two girls and a mother standing near the truck, the mother is on her cell phone. She stops and rolls down her window and ask, "is there anything wrong?" One of the girls answers, "we don't know, but this dog is locked in the truck, and it just stares out the window like it's sick or something. My mom is calling the police."

An hour later a Sheriff's deputy arrives, he recognizes the truck and radios back to his office. "Four to base, go ahead is the response, will you call Carl Warrens wife, see if she knows where he is? His truck is up here locked and idling, his dog still inside." He turns to the mother and girls and tells them, "you can go on now, I know the man that owns this truck, I'm sure everything will be fine." They get in their mini van and proceed on to the girls camp. Back on the radio the officer is told that Carl's wife said he did not return from the cabin and that she suspects he slept up there last night. "Ok, will you ask Sheriff Lynn if he can come up. I don't like the looks of this, Carl wouldn't lock his dog in his truck like this, something is a miss."

Twenty minutes later the Sheriff arrives, "what's up Bill. I can't send you out on a simple abandoned truck call?" "No Sheriff, this is Carl Warren's truck, I know him, he loves that dog, he'd never leave her in his truck like that." "Well, let's let the dog out and see if she can find Carl!" "Trucks locked," said Bill. "Well, use your tool to open it." "Gawd, look at the interior of that truck, dog chewed it to pieces," said the Sheriff! "I know, and I know that dog, Lu, she's a good dog, she'd never do that to Carl's truck," replied Bill. As they popped the lock and opened the back door of the truck, the dog bolted straight across the road and through the log fence, howling like a hound dog tracking a fox. The Sheriff said to his deputy, "well, find the dog and you'll probably find Carl, likely sitting out there having an Alzheimer's moment." Just as he finished the sentence, he could hear the dog had stopped and was howling from a stationary position. Well, that didn't take long said Sheriff Lynn. The two men began to walk out toward the dog, some 250 yards out in the aspen forest.

As they approached the dog, the deputy cried out, "my God! Sheriff, get over here quick!" It was a torso, the lower part of a torso with one leg and entrails attached. The men starred at the human remains intently, with the dog circling sniffing the ground frantically. "My God! What could have done this," said the Sheriff. "Get back to the radio, have Marty call that forensic squad in Salt Lake, get them down here immediately. What the hell has happened here? That is Carl, you think?" Asked the Sheriff. "I don't know Sheriff, I don't want to think about it," said Bill. "Carl was a good man, my God what could have done this?" The Sheriff took a deep breath and said, "I don't know Bill, we may have a grizzly up here. Get on the radio, get those forensic folks down here, I'll tape off the area."

Back at his squad car the Sheriff spoke sternly to his secretary, "I don't care Marty, we've got human remains up here, get those damn people down here or patch me through on the radio." "Just a minute Sheriff," said the secretary. "Here you go Sheriff, you're on the phone with Captain Johnson, head of the forensics department." The Sheriff spoke into the radio, "Jim?" "Yes Sheriff Lynn, I understand you have a situation down there." "Situation Jim? My god I've never seen anything like it, it's a leg with guts still attached. Get down here!" "Alright Sheriff, my team is out on a domestic violence murder case right now, I'll send them down in the morning." "Morning hell, replied the Sheriff. You get them down here now!" "I'll do what I can Sheriff, as quick as I can." "Thank you Jim. Marty?" "Yes Sheriff." "Call the University of Utah, see if you can get that bear specialist they've got, that biology Professor that did that study on Yellowstone Grizzlies, see if you can get him on the phone and call me back right away." "Yes Sheriff."

Back at the remains of the body, the dog had stopped circling and was now laying down, starring at the remains, making low whining noises. "That dog is crying," said Bill. Sheriff Lynn kneeled down next to her and said, "come on old girl, let's get you home to mom, dads gone, dads gone." He carried the small beagle back to his squad car, put her in the back seat and told the deputy, "stay here, have Marty call Donald Brown, see if he's willing to bring his dogs up. In the mean time get some back up, we guard that leg until forensics get here." The Sheriff drove off, knowing the pain he was about to inflict upon Sherry Warren, Carl's wife. She was 72 years old and as sweet as they come. It was not something he ever imagined he would have to do, on this day in his town.

At the Warren house, the Sheriff had the dog on a leash, he knocked on the door. Carl Warren's wife answered and was immediately visibly shaken. "Where is he," she asked. "Come on Sherry, let's sit down." They entered the small living room and sat down on the older couch and love seat. "Where is he Sheriff? Did he have a heart attack! I told him that damn mountain would get the best of him Sheriff," she said through flowing tears. "No, Sherry, I don't think he had a heart attack, but he's missing Sherry." "Missing, what do you mean missing?" "Sherry, we found some remains, we believe it's Carl but I can't say until forensics get here." "Can't say? Remains?

What? What do you mean remains? I want to go!"
"No, you can't go up there Sherry, you just can't,
please wait here, it's not good. I don't think Carl is
coming back." "Not coming back? I don't
understand," she said through sobbing tears.
"Please Sherry, let me call the church, have some
family come over. Let me call your daughter." "Oh
Sheriff, why, why did he have to go up there. I
sensed it, I knew it late last night, something was
wrong, I knew he was gone, I just knew it." "Help
me," the Sheriff said, "help me Sherry, help me call
your daughter, your bishop."

The Sheriff stayed with Mrs. Warren until her Bishop
arrived. Information was exchanged, the daughter
was called, the Sheriff gave Mrs. Warren a hug and a
kiss on her forehead, "be strong Sherry, your
daughter needs you to be strong." He knelt down
and gave a pat to the old beagle, "that's a good dog
you've got there Sherry, a really good dog, be good
to her." There was no response, the Sheriff looked at
the bishop, nodded his head and walked out of the
house.

What is it?

Chapter 2

Donald Brown stood looking at the severed torso and leg. He shook his head and said, "that's not a cat, Sheriff". Donald was a local, he was a mountain lion hunting guide. Hunters came from all over the world to hunt cougar in the central Utah mountains. Several world class cougars had been taken by Donald's clients. He was the most well known guide and outfitter in the area. He had hounds and horses and a life time of experience hunting cougar. Donald shook his head again and looked at the Sheriff, "I don't know Sheriff, that's like nothing I've ever seen. That's been bit in half in one bite. There's no tearing marks, no bite radius, no teeth marks, something bit that man in half in one bite, and that something ain't no cougar." The Sheriff looked at the ground, "what do you think it is Donald? A Griz?" "My gawd it would have to be one hell of a Griz! Has anyone checked for tracks?" "No", the Sheriff said, "other than deputies, you're the first one here." "Well, something this big shouldn't be hard to track, let's take a look," said Donald.

The two men started walking toward the east, deeper in the aspen groves. "Look at this Sheriff, see how the ground is all tore up? And it's more than a foot wide, my boot is a size 12. And over here, the same with the other hind leg, damn, this thing is as big as a horse! Look at that span between the hind legs, it's four feet across!" "Yeah but what is it Donald?" "I don't know, the ground is too tore up." A third man walked up from behind and joined them, it was Dr. Ronald Dreyfus from the University. "Hello gentlemen, I'm Dr. Dreyfus from the University of Utah's zoology department, I was in Las Vegas at a conference when I got a call that said it was urgent." "Good to meet you Doc," said the Sheriff, as he extended his hand. "Yes, I saw the body or what's left of it. I can almost tell you now, for certain gentlemen, that's not a grizzly attack." "No, I told the Sheriff the same thing," said Donald, extending his hand to greet the professor. "Then what is it gentlemen? I need to know and I need to know now," said the Sheriff. "I've got a girls camp two miles away with teenage girls in it, they've traveled from all over to be here, if I need to close that camp I need to know right now!"

"Have you seen any tracks," asked the professor? "That's what we're looking for now, check this out," said Donald. "My word exclaimed the professor, this animal would have to weigh 800 pounds to scar the ground like that in one stride." "Yes, I'd say at least 800, that looks more like a four wheel drive truck tore that ground up, not an animal." Said Donald. "Indeed it does! Are we sure we're dealing with an animal and not some satanic cult group?" Asked the Professor. The Sheriff looked up and said, "we are not sure of anything just yet," as he strode off further to the east.

The two men joined the Sheriff looking for tracks. "Look, look at this Donald," the Sheriff yelled toward Donald who was 30 yards off. The three men gathered and stared at what appeared to be a track in a bare spot of ground. "That's a cougar track Donald," said the Sheriff. "Yeah, so it seems," said Donald. "But it's four times bigger than anything I've ever seen. It's 14 inches across." "Indeed." Said the professor, "while it's not complete, the shape is more a cougar than anything else." "So what do we have here, a giant cat? It's got to be a hoax," said the Sheriff, "there's no such thing as a god damned giant cat, cougars don't get as big as horses!" "Then what bit that man in half Sheriff?" Asked Donald! "I don't know but its not some damn monster. It's got to be some evil sons of bitches trying to make us think it's a monster. God damn it Donald!" Yelled Sheriff Lynn. "Get your dogs and let's hunt these bastards down. There's got to be a scent they will pick up on." "Ok Sheriff, give me a day to get my gear up here, I assume the County is going to pick up the cost, right?" "Of course," the Sheriff said, "just be up here seven A.M. tomorrow morning, two horses, we're going to get to the bottom of this."

As the men walked back to the road, they could see the Salt Lake County forensics team at the remains.

"Good afternoon Sheriff, I'm." "I know who you are," interrupted the Sheriff, "I called you in. We've got a mess here Jim, a real mess. I've got teenage girls at camp two miles from here and two experts telling me I've got some kind of a damn monster cat roaming these woods. That's just bullshit! Can you tell me what I've got here, Jim, what did this?" "Well Sheriff, it's almost as if this man has been cut in half with a serrated edged knife, a very large knife, the cut is clean, the bones more cut than crushed, no hacking or chewing marks. We're taking tissue samples that we will test for DNA. If an animal did this we will know." "How long is that going to take?"Asked the Sheriff. "A week, possibly 10 days." "No, no it's not Jim, I don't have a week, I need to know now," yelled the Sheriff. "I can expedite the order at the state lab Sheriff but it just depends on the priority, I can't promise but maybe in 3-4 days." Professor Dreyfus spoke up, "if you can get me samples we can do DNA testing in our lab, at the University." "Of course, I'll have them double the sampling, it will be a good cross check, if we're looking at something unusual." "Unusual?" Said the Sheriff, "I haven't seen anything usual, yet. Donald! Seven AM tomorrow morning." "You got it Sheriff!" Said Donald as he walked to his truck.

No Human Could Do This
Chapter 3

Donald and the Sheriff were back on the mountain 6:30 am the next morning. The horses unloaded, their hooves nervously stamping the ground in front of them, their breath steaming in the crisp morning air. Donald brought six of his hounds, the Sheriff and

Donald led them on leash over to where the torso had laid. The dogs started howling and pulling to get off leash. "That's it Sheriff, they've got the scent, turn them loose." The dogs were released and they headed off into the woods towards the north east. Donald and the Sheriff hurried back to the horses to mount and give chase. "I don't know Sheriff, those dogs are lion dogs, they reacted exactly as they do when they're tracking a lion, I don't think they're chasing people." "Well let's go Donald, see what we've got."   On the horses moving briskly through the aspens, a half hour later they found themselves at the girls camp, where two camp counselors and several girls had been interrupted by six hounds howling as they ran through the camp. The startled girls watched as their Native American arts and crafts projects were brought to an abrupt halt. "What's going on," a camp counselor yelled to the two men on horses. The Sheriff stopped and said, "nothing, nothing to worry about we're just working some dogs, sorry for the interruption." Donald looked at the Sheriff and shook his head. The Sheriff replied, "we don't want to start a panic. We need to know what we're dealing with before I order this camp closed."

Two hours into the hunt, the exhausted men stopped the horses and dismounted. Donald looked at the Sheriff and said, "I don't know Sheriff, these dogs are moving at break neck speed, they're my best dogs, they've usually got a cougar treed by now but they're getting away from us." The Sheriff nodded in agreement while trying to catch his breath. "What will we do if we lose them?" "I've got GPS collars on them, we can track them down." The hunt went on, they had dropped into the valley three thousand feet below, crossed the highway and headed back up the mountain toward the ski resort. By three in the afternoon they had lost the dogs, they could no longer hear them. Donald pulled out his GPS unit and said, "they're still tracking, they're headed south of the ski resort toward Radar Peak, that's near twelve thousand foot elevation. Listen Sheriff, we're 20 miles from the trucks, if we head back now, follow the highway back, we'll get to the trucks at dark. I can monitor the GPS tonight, when they stop, we'll have our cougar treed and we can return in the morning." "Alright Donald, let's head back, I won't be able to walk for two days, I haven't spent this much time on a horse since I was a teenager." They turned the horses back down the mountain toward the valley, the highway and the stream along side of it.

As they rode along the side of the highway the Sheriff told Donald, "this is not good, I've got the ski resort on one side of the valley and the girls camp on the other, whatever this is, it went right through both, and it ain't no human, there is no way trucks, motorcycles, ATVs or any human covered the ground we did today." "I told you Sheriff, those dogs are on a lion, they don't track people like that." "Well, we've got to kill that damn lion Donald, I can't have something like that roaming this mountain, walking right through a girls camp unnoticed in the middle of the night. I can't have this."

The two men arrived at their trucks well after dark, both exhausted. "Check that GPS Donald," said the Sheriff. "They've gone further south," Donald said, "they're past Radar Peak, near the lava fields to the east, and they're still moving, they must be in the lava fields, they're moving much slower." "Or maybe they're worn out like us," the Sheriff said. "No, these are my best dogs, they'll run till they drop, day or night, they can go for two days, maybe three before they slow down, no something has slowed them down, I think they're in the lava fields." "Ok Donald, thanks" the Sheriff said as he guided his horse up into the trailer. "You want me to help you with these horses tonight? Don't put them up wet." "No, I won't Sheriff, we will see where the dogs are in the morning and decide what to do then." "Ok" said the Sheriff, "my phone will be on all night, call me if you see any change." "I will, good night." "Good night Donald, thanks for your help, I wish it was a good night but I fear it aint!"

With that the two men got in their trucks and drove down the mountain. The Sheriff put his in tow/haul mode to get the engine braking down the hill, he knew he was too tired to safely drive down that mountain. He picked up his cell and called his wife Christine . "Thank god you're safe," she said. "Did you kill it," she asked? "No the Sheriff said, we never saw anything, the dogs were too fast for us to keep up." "What are you going to do now?" She asked. "Come home and get into bed with you, I'm so tired I can hardly walk." "We'll get home. I'll have some supper ready. You need to get this thing, whoever or whatever it is." "Yes," he replied. "Donald thinks it's a lion, his dogs reacted to lion scent." "Well I don't want you up there with that thing roaming around." She said. He replied, "I have to dear, it's my job, you know that." With that they ended the call and the Sheriff stared ahead into the headlight beams of his truck. A deer darted out from the side of the road, the Sheriff was too slow to respond and his truck just clipped the hind quarters of the deer. Hell he thought, what else tonight. He didn't stop but drove on, to the waiting arms of his wife and a hot bowl of beef stew.

We've Got Nothing
Chapter 4

The phone rang at 5:30 am. The Sheriff rolled out of bed and answered it, "what have you got Donald?" "I've got nothing Sheriff! Nothing! I've got thousands of dollars in hounds and GPS equipment suddenly gone! Like they dropped off the earth! The last hit was 3:48 this morning, then nothing! That was in the lava fields, toward the back, the east end up against that cliff." "There's that lava tube up there," said the Sheriff, "that cave supposedly no one has ever been able to find the back of, they could have gone in there." "Yes," said Donald, "that would block the GPS signal." "So what do you want to do Donald?" "I don't know Sheriff, we can't ride horses into that lava field and it's too tough a hike for you or me." "True," said the Sheriff. "I can get the Salt Lake County helicopter down here, we've got an agreement to use it when needed, I'd say we need it, but before I call that in Donald, I want to give your dogs a little more time. What will they do if they don't find anything." "Well Sheriff, they'll, return to where we started. I left one of my jackets up there, they'll come to that jacket and stay there, but they won't for a couple days." "Ok, well, let me call Salt Lake this morning and arrange that helicopter, probably for tomorrow if it's not already scheduled out. In the mean time keep an eye on that GPS and call me the second you see any movement." "Yes Sheriff I will, those dogs are hell on a mountain lion, they've fought many before, but this ain't no mountain lion Sheriff." "Well don't be so quick to jump to conclusions Donald, we don't know what we've got yet. Until proven otherwise, I've got to believe it's not something out of the ordinary. It might be a cat, a big one, but until I see it, I have to believe it's a mountain lion or a bear, I can't assume it's something else until proven that it is." "Well Sheriff, I don't know how much more proof you need other than that leg and those tracks, but it's your business so I'll follow your lead." "Thanks Donald, I appreciate that, maybe it's too many years with too many lawyers and judges doubting what I bring them, but it is what it is, until proven otherwise." With that the two men hung up. The Sheriff returned to the bedroom where his wife said, "come back to bed." She was a beautiful woman, even at her age men noticed, he looked at her shapely form and thought about it, then said, no, I've got to catch this cat. I can't send all those girls home from camp, or close that ski resort and their summer mountain bike income, I've got to catch this cat. With that he stepped into the bathroom and shower in preparation for the days work.

"Call on line three Sheriff," Marty, a 32 year old divorced secretary said over the intercom. "Who is it," he asked. "I don't know Sheriff, I forgot to ask." This annoyed the Sheriff visibly, he had discussed this many times with her to no avail. But he didn't fire her, really he couldn't, the labor pool in Cedar City Utah was very limited and what he'd get to replace her would probably be worse. Besides, she was cute, nicely filled out a pair of jeans and was occasionally flirtatious, which helped to pass the time in what was on most other days, a boring job consisting of traffic accidents, domestic disputes, the town drunks and an occasional gas station robbery.

The Sheriff picked up the phone. "Hello! Sheriff this is Dr. Dreyfus from the University, we met on the mountain a couple days ago?" "Yes Doctor, how are you?" "Fine, fine, and you Sheriff?" "Doing well, was his response. What do you have Professor?" "Well, I must say, these tissue samples the state lab provided are quite intriguing." "How so?" the Sheriff asked. "Well, they're definitely in the lion family but they don't match the North American cougar." "Really, well what do they match." "That's the problem Sheriff, they don't match any living species of cat!" "Well again, what do they match?" "Nothing Sheriff, that's what I'm saying, nothing!" "So what do we have, some new species of cat on the mountain?" asked Sheriff Lynn. "I don't know Sheriff, I'll wait for the state labs results and cross check with them but if they come up with the same result, and I have no reason to suspect they won't, but if they have what I have, then the only place left to look is the fossil record." "Fossil record?" "Yes, prehistoric cats that have gone extinct. We have genetic samples taken from prehistoric fossils, the Saber Tooth Tiger for example, that has been extinct for at least ten thousand years. I'm thinking we may be dealing with something along those lines, the South American tiger weighed as much as a thousand pounds and was much larger than modern tigers." "Ah, doctor I don't mean to be rude but how do I explain to Carl Warren's wife that her husband was killed by a tiger from South America that's been dead for ten thousand years?" "You don't Sheriff, I'm just trying to give you some insight into what we are going to research here, this DNA is definitely lion but we can't match it. So we have to start somewhere, the fossil record will give us some clues to what we may have on that mountain." "Bull shit Doc! I need real answers, not clues and I need them now." "Well I'm sorry, but we're doing the best we can, there is no modern living cat with a DNA match to the samples we took on the mountain, yet it is a cat." "And you're sure of that Doc, Carl Warren was killed by some kind of lion?" Asked the Sheriff. "Yes, there was extensive DNA in the bite wound, it's a lion." "Ok, well I guess that's a start. We've got hound dogs on it now, they acted as if they were tracking a cougar, so I guess the dogs agree with you." "Yes Sheriff, that makes sense, the dogs are bred to alert to specific animals, and those cougar hounds would respond to most breeds of cat. But there is one other thing Sheriff, we've seen this in smaller animals in central Utah, frogs, fish, some birds." "Seen what Doc? Genetic mutations," the Professor replied. "Central Utah was down wind of the nuclear testing the government did in the fifties and sixties. That fall out has a ten thousand year half life, it's still active in those hills, it's modifying the genetic codes of all sorts of animals and trees. We've been monitoring this for decades." "And what does that have to do with our cat," the Sheriff asked. "Well, we may have a genetic mutation of a modern cougar, which is an indirect descendant of the prehistoric saber tooth tiger line of cats." "Wonderful" the Sheriff sighed. "I've got some mutant giant tiger roaming the girls camp at night." "Well, let's not jump to conclusions Sheriff, but that is a distinct possibility we are looking into here at the University. This could be a tremendous scientific find for our department!" "Well, you'll excuse me if I don't join your exuberance Doc but I've got a good man dead, a half dozen hounds chasing some mutant cat to hell and back and hundreds of people on the mountain that I have to protect." "I understand Sheriff, we each have our jobs to do. Once I get the state lab results, we will consult with them and continue our work in trying to identify what you're dealing with. In the mean time just know, yes, you've got a dangerous animal on that mountain, and no it's not a bear, it's a lion of considerable size and strength. If your going to chase it you'd better be prepared to kill it. Make sure you're loaded for bear, as the saying goes, and I mean that literally, bring the biggest weapons you've got." "We're way ahead of you on that Doc, but thanks for the advise. We've got a GPS track up to the lava fields north east of Radar Peak. We're going to take a helicopter up there and see what's become of our hounds, tomorrow afternoon. You're welcome to come along, it's just me and a local tracker. We leave from the airport at noon." "Thank you Sheriff, I'll be at the airport at noon, I'll bring some camera equipment if in fact we get a look at this lion." "Alright Doc, see you tomorrow then."

The Sheriff looked up at Marty who was listening to the conversation. "What on earth are you talking about Sheriff? Giant tigers on the mountain?" "No, no Marty, that's just a University Professor trying to generate interest in his program, get some additional grant money. We're chasing a cougar, nothing more." "Are you sure Sheriff? I've got a friend with a daughter at that girls camp." "Sure as shooting Marty." She leaned down placing her hands on his desk, looking into his eyes, "you're not lying to me are you Sheriff?" He avoided looking at her cleavage and up into her eyes, "I'm just trying to do my job

Marty. And don't you say a word to anybody about this you hear! We don't want to start a needless panic. Those people working at that ski resort need this summer income. The girls at that camp look forward to it all year. We are not going to ruin their fun over some silly rumors now are we Marty?" "No Sheriff, I guess not," she blinked her eyes intentionally, he looked away, avoiding her loose shirt and tight jeans. She stood up and walked to the door, turning back over her shoulder she said, "you know Sheriff, you can tell me the truth, you don't need to hide things from me, carry that burden all by yourself." "I know Marty, let's just keep our heads down, deal with the facts we have and do our job." She smiled and walked into the other room. He thought of his wife, he thought of Marty how young and willing she was and of how many men he knew that had ruined their marriages with that mistake. He was not going to make that mistake. He might have to fire Marty.

Carnage

Chapter 5

The Bell Jet Ranger helicopter howled loudly on the landing pad as three men ran toward it. The Sheriff, Donald Brown with his GPS tracking unit and a .50 caliber long rifle in hand and Professor Dreyfus with a camera bag, camera strapped over his shoulder and his biological sampling kit. Once strapped in with head sets in place, the pilot asked, "where to?" The Sheriff sitting in the right front seat said, "see that peak?" "Yes," replied the pilot. "Over that peak and then about five miles to the southeast to a lava field." "You've got it!" Replied the pilot. "Donald!" Yelled the Sheriff. "Yes sir!" "Turn that GPS on, let me know immediately if you get a hit." "It's already on Sheriff, nothing since Tuesday morning." Turning back to the pilot the Sheriff said, "on the southeast end of that lava field is a ridge, we'd like you to put us down on that ridge and wait for our return, shouldn't be more than thirty minutes or an hour." "You've got all day Sheriff Lynn, said the pilot. Nothing else is booked for the day, short of an emergency you can take all the time you want."

The helicopter buffeted in the strong wind as it crossed over Radar Peak at 15,000 feet. "Now, see that lava field off to the left?" Said the Sheriff. "Yes sir," replied the pilot, "head for that," turning to the back seat, the Sheriff asked, "anything on the GPS yet Donald?" "No, not yet, if they're in that lava tube we won't get a signal, the ground will block it." "Alright Sheriff, where do you want me to put you down?" The Sheriff turned back to Donald and asked, "do you remember where the entrance to that cave is?" "I don't know Sheriff, I've never seen it from the air, can we run up and down the ridge for a minute?" "Sure" the pilot replied, "let me know when you see it." Just then the GPS beeped. "I've got a hit Sheriff! My dogs! They're just up to the right!" Said Donald. The pilot maneuvered the helicopter along the steep ridge to the right. "That's it! They're just below us." All the men looked out below but could see nothing but large car sized black lava rocks. "See that clearing to the left?" Yes replied the pilot. "Can you set us down there?" "I'll try Sheriff," said the pilot, "but the wind is stiff, 20 gusting to 30 knots, I might have to keep it running to maintain stability." "Ok! If you'll let us out there we will be quick as we can." "You've got it." The pilot edged perilously close to the steep terrain, trying to land on the one semi flat spot in the area. "It's too steep" said the pilot, "I can't put it down there, but I can put one skid on that rock and hover if you guys can climb out." The Sheriff nodded in agreement. As the men started to climb out the pilot said, "I'll hover about a quarter mile out, watch this rock, when you're ready, climb back on this rock and I'll pick you up, I've got about 90 minutes of fuel left." "Alright," yelled the Sheriff, "watch for us." The two men looked at each other in agreement. The helicopter arched back out over the lava field as the three men stood on the rock and watched. "What does that GPS say?" Yelled the Sheriff. "To the right," yelled Donald.

The three men climbed down into the large black colored rocks as if on a deer hunt, excited to find this animal but having no idea of the life altering event that awaited them. "This isn't the lava tube Donald!" Yelled the Sheriff! "No, it's not, but it must be a side entrance, or another I've never heard of before." The men climbed about 150 feet over and around the large rocks when the Professor yelled look! Off to the left, one of Donald's hounds. It was dead, disemboweled. The dog apparently having dragged itself out of the cave and died. Donald, rushing to the dogs side, "oh Missy, Missy, why the hell did I let you go on this! God damn it Missy, what did I do to you?" "Donald" Yelled the Sheriff! "Get a hold of yourself, we've got to kill whatever did that to your dog!" Donald looked up with rage in his face, "you're fucking right about that Sheriff," With tears welling up in his eyes, Donald rose to his feet, chambered a shell in his fifty caliber rifle and started into the cave. The Professor put a head lamp on his forehead and handed one to the Sheriff. The two men followed Donald into the cave.

Inside the cave it was quiet, the sound of the wind and helicopter gone. "Look Sheriff" said Donald, "more signals now, Max is about 50 feet ahead, Toby is about a quarter mile further in the cave." The men walked silently further into the cave, the audible beeps of the GPS unit we're loud now. The Sheriff stopped and looked down to his right, the severed head of a hound dog, with a GPS collar still attached to its neck. "Donald!" Said the Sheriff, pointing toward the dogs remains. Donald approached, "thats Max Sheriff," said Donald as he bent down to see the face of his dog. "Max and Missy were a breeding pair, the four others their pups. This fucking cat dies today!" Said Donald with a crazed rage in his eyes. The two men looked at each other and continued into the cave. Just then the GPS signaled Toby was on the move, approaching them. "Toby is still alive Sheriff, he's trying to reach us!" Immediately there was a loud hissing blast of air, like the release of the air brakes of a commercial diesel truck. It was the threatening sound of a large cat, Donald knew the sound well. "Come to me you son of a bitch, I'll kill your god damned ass, right fucking here and right fucking now you piece of shit," screamed Donald. Pandemonium broke out inside the cave. The Professor froze in fear and amazement at the sound of the enormous lion. Donald was in full adrenaline driven rage as the Sheriff tried to gather the two men to get them out of the cave.   The GPS signal was approaching, Donald fired shots into the dark, the powerful rifle ricocheting bullets off the rock walls of the cave. "Donald!" Yelled the Sheriff, "get out of here, you'll kill us all!" Donald stumbled back in the realization of the danger and started to run toward the cave opening. A second deafening hissing sound rang out in the cave followed by a terrifying screaming growl. The Sheriff grabbed the collar of the Professor trying to drag him out of the cave. The Professor frozen in fear, fell backward as the two men fell to the cave floor. As the Sheriff stood back up he saw two slanted eyes reflecting in the dark headed toward him, eyes spread wide and well above his eye level. He screamed, "Professor! Professor! Get out! Get out! Get out now!" Screaming as he ran back toward the cave entrance, get out! Get out! Within fifty feet of day light he could see Donald standing at the entrance with his rifle pointed back into the cave. The Professor was still in the cave. Deep from within the cave came the scream of blood curdling horror, the dark beast was upon the Professor, he was being torn apart alive, in the darkness of the cave. Donald fired shots back into the dark, emptying his large caliber rifle into the terrifying screams and horror of the blackness.

The Sheriff, not breaking stride grabbed Donald's arm and the two men scrambled back up the rocks to the helicopter already hovering over the rock. Donald threw open the door and the two men climbed over each other while screaming, "go! Go! Go! Get out of here!" The pilot, stunned by what he saw, his training took over and he held the helicopter in place until the men were fully inside. "Go!" Screamed the Sheriff, "Go!" The helicopter banked away in the strong wind. "The other man! The Professor, where is he?" Yelled the pilot! "He won't be coming back!" Yelled the Sheriff, "now get out of here!" The pilot banked the helicopter sharply off to the right where he cleared the trees and ridge and returned to a hover about 200 yards off the ridge. "Sheriff," he yelled into his head set. "We can't leave that man behind!" "That man isn't a man any more," yelled the Sheriff! "Now get us out of here, back to the airport." The pilot regaining his composure checked his instruments, he purposely flew the aircraft at its highest speed toward the Cedar City airport. He yelled to his passengers, "what happened back there?" The Sheriff put on his head set and answered, "I don't know, I don't know what happened." "What do you mean you don't know, sir!" The pilot was a war veteran and he understood rank, he knew the Sheriff was the ranking officer in the aircraft and he honored that rank, but he also had lived by the motto "no man left behind". So he pressed the question to the Sheriff. The Sheriff said, "we were attacked, attacked by something in the dark, the Professor froze and I could not get him out. What ever it was killed the Professor, of that I am certain." "My god," said the pilot. "What do you mean something?" "Some kind of cat," said the Sheriff, "some kind of big lion" The pilot sensing the trauma the two men had just experienced, ceased his questioning and concentrated on his flying. Donald looked at the Sheriff, with tears in his eyes he said, "my dog Sheriff, Toby was trying to get to me!" Donald starred out the window of the helicopter, tears streaming down his cheeks. The Sheriff replied. "No, no he wasn't Donald, that dog is gone, it's GPS is in the belly of that cat and that is how we're going to kill it!"

The helicopter touched down at the Cedar City airport. The pilot kept it running and stated, "I'll be filing a report on this, one of my passengers died, I have to file a report on this." "Yes I know," said the Sheriff. "Call me later if you need help with the report, have Sheriff Clark call me. I'm going to need some help with this." "You've got it sir!" With that the helicopter took off to the North headed back to Salt Lake City. The Sheriff and Donald walked back to their trucks. "Listen Donald, not a word about this to anybody you hear? We've got to keep this under control or more lives will be lost in the panic and craziness that naturally follows events like this. Remember when that bear killed that kid up in Duck Creek?" "Yes," said Donald. "Well, we had a man shot in one of those hunting parties, idiots from California came and shot up cabins in the area wildly shooting through the woods. We can't have that again. We've got to kill that animal and keep it quiet while we do it or this place will get out of control! Do you understand Donald?" "Yes Sheriff, I understand. But what shall I say, to my wife, family, friends who will want to know where my dogs are?" "Just tell them you ran into a nasty cat and lost some dogs, that's all they need to know right now. I'll give you a call later when I figure out what our next step is." "Ok Sheriff. I'm sorry I lost my cool in there, I've lost dogs to cougar before but this group were more than dogs, I became attached to them and that's something a hunter should never do." Said Donald. "I know," replied Sheriff Lynn. "And I'm sorry about your dogs, I know you loved them. The county will reimburse you when this is all over." Donald looked down, "I've got friends Sheriff, with dogs and horses, now we know where that beast is hold up, we can kill it, we can smoke it out and kill it." "I don't know that we can Donald, this is what that Professor said it was, some kind of monster cat, the thing is huge, I saw it's eyes, it's like nothing I've ever seen before and I've never been scared like that before, never in my life. But listen Donald, I've got to get back to the office, keep this quiet and we will talk tomorrow." "Ok Sheriff," Donald walked forward and hugged the Sheriff, "thank you Sheriff, thank you for getting me out of there." "You bet Donald, I only wish I could have got the Professor out of there." "I know Sheriff, I know, it's not your fault, he froze, you couldn't have got him out, you did what you could do. I saw it, I'll be your witness if I need to." "Thanks" said Sheriff Lynn.

Marty looked up as the Sheriff walked in with blood on his forehead and a torn shirt. "My god what happened to you Sheriff!" He ignored her and walked in back into his office. "We lost a man on the mountain Marty." "Lost a man?" "Yes, he's gone. Don't answer questions from the media, refer them to Sheriff Clark up in Salt Lake County." "Ok Sheriff, your heads cut, let me see that!" "No, let it be." She walked into the bathroom, got some hydrogen peroxide and paper towels. "Your heads cut, it's bleeding." She started to clean the wound, "please, don't Marty." "Hush Jeff, I'm going to take care of you." He leaned back and let her dress the wound. "What happened?" She asked. "We had a problem in a cave, I hit my head." She took his face in her hands, "now you tell me Sheriff! I have a right to know!" He sighed, "Marty I've got enough on my plate, please help me, please be on my team. I am the county Sheriff, you know that, help me!" She pulled a chair up and sat directly in front of him. "I am with you Jeff, you know that, you feel that, you helped me and now I'm here for you." "I know Marty, I know, just, let me be for a minute, it was hard, it was hard up there, I need a minute." She leaned forward, kissed his forehead, put his face in her hands and said, "I'm here, I'm here and you know it." He nodded his head, as she stood up and walked to the door, he watched her, but instead of being attracted to her, he was comforted, felt as if she was someone he could confide in. He leaned back in his chair, took a deep breath, leaned forward and grabbed the phone to call Sheriff Clark in Salt Lake and advise him as to the fate and last known location of the body of Professor Dreyfus, The Department Head of the School of Zoology at the University of Utah.

A Beautiful Woman

Chapter 6

"ZOOLOGY PROFESSOR KILLED BY ANCIENT TIGER" read the head lines of the Salt Lake Tribune. "What the hell! Can you believe this," Sheriff Jeff Lynn said to his wife of 30 years, Christine. He slammed the paper down on the kitchen table. "What kind of idiots do they have up there in Salt Lake." "Well, what did you tell Sheriff Clark?" Asked Christine "I didn't tell him this! I said it was a cat, a lion, but I didn't see it in the dark, I couldn't see it! They must have interviewed one of those graduate students working on the DNA match. Those are the only people who knew what the theory was on the research. I'll have to order the ski resort closed, the girls camp closed, I have to do it now, it would be irresponsible if I didn't. Damn it, you know, you tell people to keep things quite, to avoid panic and this is what you get!" "Well Jeff, you can't leave those girls up there with this thing roaming around at night."

"The girls sleep in those metal storage containers, they're safe at night. Regardless, now the parents and church leaders are going to be on me. I'll have to close it and ruin those kids summer. And the ski resort, that was sold last year to that California group, that's going to be the end of those summer jobs for a lot of kids in this town." "Well it has to be done!" She said. "Actually dear, no it didn't, if some idiots would have kept their mouths shut! We know where this lion is now and we can kill it!" Said the Sheriff as he slammed the door on his way out to work.

Marty had her hair pulled back, the way the Sheriff liked it. "Good morning" she said as he walked into his office, "morning," he replied. "Will you look up the number for the new owners of the ski resort, they're out of California, I need to shut them down." "Actually I've got a call from them Sheriff, two people are missing up there, a young couple hiking, they didn't come home on Monday. Their parents are on the way in from L.A.". "Great! What do we know?" "Only that they rented a room at the lodge, they were due back Monday and they didn't show, their car is still in the parking lot." "Ok, will you get Joe to drive up, get a report and get back to me." "Yes." "When are the parents due in." "They didn't say, only that they were driving up today to the ski resort and wanted the police to meet them." "Ok, well have Joe talk to them and let me know if they want to see me." "Will do Sheriff. What about the girls camp and the camp grounds?" She asked. "The camp grounds are the Forest Service responsibility, call the girls camp, talk to the supervisor and see if they can set up a meeting with me. We've got to close them down. Do you know what day they do their turn around, when the new kids come up for the week." Yes, Marty said, "it's today, they have parent orientation tonight." "Great, everybody is going up today and I have to send them home. Give the camp a call and see if you can set up a meeting today, let me know, I'll drive up there." "Yes Sheriff," she stood in the doorway, in an S curve like a magazine model, she looked at him, he looked up and knew what she was doing, he closed his eyes and looked back down, he didn't need or want the distraction now but she knew, he needed it, a break from the pressure he was under, and clearly she thought, he wasn't getting it at home.

You can't close us down," yelled Jerry Kramer, the CFO of Ski America, the corporation that had just acquired the ski resort the previous year. "Actually I can" replied the Sheriff. "There is a dangerous cat on the mountain." "Dangerous cat?" Jerry replied! "We've got cougars and bears at all of our resort properties, we don't shut them down because of a little run in!" "This is no little run in sir! Two men are dead, two people are missing!" Replied the Sheriff in strong terms. "And you can't prove any of it was done by a cougar or bear near our property, it's all speculation!" Yelled back Jerry. "Listen sir, I don't want to do this anymore than you do, our kids need those jobs up there, that's how they make their money for school in the fall, we're a college town, those kids need that income. I don't want to shut them down!" "Well then, don't,"responded Jerry. "I'll get a court order preventing you, you don't have the authority to shut us down!" "In a public emergency I do, but you take your best shot and actually sir, if you do that, get a restraining order, a judge intervening would take the blame off of me if anything did happen." "I'll get the lawyers working on it right now," Jerry said. "An emergency restraining order, it's coming your way Sheriff." "Well, all legal authority aside," said the Sheriff, "there is a dangerous cat roaming that mountain, you need to protect your people, your guest. I've got a deputy on your property right now investigating a missing couple from California. I hope like hell they're just lost off in the bushes somewhere, but I fear they're not!" "Let me know what your deputy finds Sheriff," said Jerry. "I'll make sure our cougar and bear warning signs are posted on the property, we absolutely can not close down." "I'll give you 48 hours sir, absent a court order, I'm closing you down," said the Sheriff. "You'll get your order Sheriff, my best lawyers are already working on it." "Ok Jerry, you serve me with the order here in Cedar, I'll give you two days." "You've got it Sheriff!" With that the two men hung up the phone.

The Sheriff took a deep breath, looked up and Marty was standing in the doorway. "Lunch" she asked? The curve of her lower back, the firm legs, tight jeans, her beautiful hair and smile, she was one of southern Utah's finest, a beautiful woman in her prime, but she got in trouble early in life, as often happens with beautiful girls. Drugs were being dealt out of the bar where she worked, his office raided the place, he pulled Marty aside and kept her from being arrested, though he was confident she was involved in the drugs and in what some would consider prostitution. He needed a new front office person and offered her the position, trying to give her a chance at a decent life, something he felt she deserved. She accepted the job more than six months ago and was still learning the procedures of the County Sheriffs office. The job came with good benefits and salary, something she could rely upon. She was 32 and this was her first chance at a normal life. She had been through several men, men who were more interested in her as a trophy, men who were incapable of love. Young beautiful girls coming out of the poverty of small towns rarely stood a chance. He wanted to give her a chance, though he knew there would be challenges along the way, changing a life was more than changing a job, he had to change her environment and the way she thought about herself. For now, all he could do was try to set an example.

As Marty stood in the door way, her beauty on full display, he considered his decision to bring her into the office and questioned his own motives. He contemplated her lunch offer, knowing it was a loaded question. He thought about the last time he made love to his wife, the perfunctory nature of it, the lack of passion. He looked up and shook his head, he told Marty "no, I've got to get up to the girls camp. Did you get them on the phone?" He asked. "No, Marty said, there's something wrong with the phone line, it rings busy every time I call." "Ok, well I'm going to drive up. Do you know where those closed by order of Sheriff signs are, the ones we used on that bar last year?" They're still in the storage unit Sheriff." "Ok, well I'm going to grab those and some tape, head up to the mountain." She stepped in front of him as he walked out the door. He looked at her, "please Marty, I can't." She put her hand on his chest and said, "you can." He pushed her hand away. "I can't Marty, I really can't, you know that, please, I can't." She smiled and let him pass, believing she had broken the ice and it was now only a matter of time. In his truck, he stopped, took a deep breath, what am I going to do he thought. I want her but I can't, I just can't, gawd what a mess that would be, I've got to fire her.

He grabbed the radio, "1 to 4, Joe, are you at the ski resort?" "Just pulling in Sheriff what's up." "Joe, we've got a dangerous cat on the mountain, those people up there need to know. I don't know if this has anything to do with that missing couple but make sure that manager knows, make sure he's got his cougar and bear warning signs out, tell him to cancel night runs, shut the lights down on the mountain so people can't be mountain biking on the hill at night. Do what you can, they're going to get a court order stopping us from closing them down but until we get that cat, we can't have people out on the mountain at night. Do what you can, ask the manager to cooperate, we can't force the issue, they've already got lawyers involved. I'll be over at the girls camp, when I'm done there I'll drive over to the ski resort. If the parents of that missing couple show up, don't say anything about the cat, just tell them I'll be there as soon as I can." Joe replied, "got it Sheriff, 4 out."

He turned off the highway and onto the narrow road headed up to the top of the mountain, the tight switch backs kept his mind off Marty, off the cat and on the road, which was a welcome relief. Pulling up to the girls camp he saw vehicles lining the road, what the hell he thought. Pulling into the gate he saw a large aspen laying across the road, it had taken out the phone and electrical lines into the property. Walking toward the camp host trailer, the camp host came out and said, "Sheriff, I'm so glad to see you here!" "What's up with the tree" asked the Sheriff? "I can't start my chain saw Sheriff and I can't get out of the property to take it to the shop to get it fixed." "Hell" said the Sheriff! "Where is it?" "Over here," the two men walked toward a picnic table where a small chain saw sat in a puddle of oil. "This saw isn't big enough for that tree. Where's the camp equipment?" "It's locked Sheriff, I took over for the last's host and he accidentally took the keys home with him. He's in Vegas, we're going to get new keys made." "What a shit show," the Sheriff said in obvious frustration "Sheriff! I'll ask you to watch your language around these girls, this is a religious camp." "I know, I'm sorry, I'm sorry, it's been a hard few days. What's your name?" "Bob, Bob Hansen. "Well Bob, we've got to get that tree off the road and the power and phone back on." "Yes sir, I know!" "Where's the camp gear storage unit?" The men walked about 100 yards toward a twenty foot steel storage unit. "Stand back Bob, we've got to shoot this lock off." Bob, an overweight man of short stature, stood back behind a tree. The Sheriff took out his 9mm service revolver put the barrel near the lock and pulled the trigger. He heard the gathering of women down at the large fire pit area yell in alarm, looking down at the lock, it wasn't off yet so he fired again. Pulling the lock off the door he opened the steel door, walked in, on a shelf was a 20 inch McCulloch chain saw. He grabbed the saw and handed it to Bob just as two women approached and yelled in a hostile tone, "what are you doing? Don't you have any better sense than to fire a gun around all these kids?"

"Ladies, I'm sorry I had to use my weapon, we've got to get that tree off the road and close this camp." "Close the camp? Why? We just got here!" "For security reasons, I'm the county Sheriff, we're going to close this camp." "What? Why?" "Ladies, I'll give you a full explanation down at the group area in a few minutes but first we've got to get that road open." He handed the saw to Bob and asked, "how long until you can get that tree off the road Bob?" "I don't know Sheriff, I've never cut up one that big and this altitude is hard on me, I just got here." The Sheriff looked at the ground and shook his head. "Are there any other men up here?" "There's a couple fathers down at the group area." The Sheriff looked down at the group area, he saw two small men talking with the mothers and girls. He walked down to them, the conversations stopped when the man in uniform approached. The Sheriff asked, "have either of you ever run a chain saw?" Both shook their heads in unison and laughed with each other and the girls and mothers. The Sheriff just stared at them and walked away, pansy assed church ladies he thought. "Well Bob," he said, "it's down to you and me, we've got to get that tree off the road."

About half the group had come up the night before to spend the first night with their daughters and get them settled in. Their cars were trapped behind the tree. "What about the power Bob," the Sheriff asked. "We've got to get the power back on, do you know if that line is hot?" "I don't Sheriff, I just roped it off to keep people away, cell phones don't work up here so we can't call an electrician." "Ok, well, let me look at it." The Sheriff walked back down to the road and fallen tree. He looked at the power line, followed it back to the pole, saw no switch box on the pole, no junction box. "Well, that line is most likely still hot he said to no one nearby. He yelled back up the hill, Bob, come down here!" Bob walked briskly down the hill with the two angry mothers in tow. "Bob" the Sheriff said, "that line is considered hot until proven otherwise." "We've got to get the power company up here. Do you have a back up generator?" "Yes." "Do you know how to run it?" "I was told the instructions were on the wall." "Ok, well, let's get a ladder and some rope, I'm going to tie that power line up on the power pole, we can't have it laying on the ground like this. Then we're going to get that tree off the road and send these people home. For now, let's get them gathered at the fire pit, I need to tell them of the situation." The Sheriff looked at the power line laying in the dirt, pinned under the tree, he thought about the rubber gloves in his truck, if they'd be sufficient insulation. He turned and looked back at the fire pit. Bob was gathering the women and girls. He thought of his wife and Marty, shook his head and walked toward the fire pit.

"Ladies," he paused, then turning to look at the three men, he said, "we've got a situation on the mountain, we need to close the camp and send you home." A sigh and some booing came from the slightly more than 100 gathered at the fire pit. "What's the situation?" asked Bob. "A man was killed, two miles from here, late last week." A hush fell over the crowd. The Sheriff looked out over the crowd, "we think he was killed by a cougar." Panicked talking began, some girls started crying. "Now! Your attention please! Please!" The crowd grew quite. "A cougar was tracked from this mountain to a spot more than 30 miles from here, it's not likely to return but we're not taking any chances. Those of you with your vehicles on the road, take your daughters and go home." Several started to walk out of the meeting at that point. "Stop," yelled the Sheriff, "there is a live power line down with that tree in the road. I need you to stay here until we secure that line." The loud talking began again and several ignored the Sheriffs request and headed for the gate. "Bob!" Yelled the Sheriff. "Will you go down to the gate and escort these people out? Keep them away from that tree and power line." "Yes sir" said Bob. "Now those of you with cars inside the camp, please be patient, we are trying to clear the road so you can leave. There is no immediate danger, so please relax and go about your business until we clear the road. But please, don't wander outside of the camp. We will clear the road as soon as possible." The crowd began talking very loudly, the majority gathered their things and headed down the hill to their cars on the road. A group of about thirty remained, 12 adult women and the rest teenage girls, the two other men had left. An attractive 40 year old woman approached the Sheriff. "I'm Rachel Stewart, I'm the assigned leader for most this group, is there anything we can do to help you?" "Yes, please, thank you for stepping forward. Just keep everyone together, keep them occupied, busy, Bob and I will get you out of here as soon as we can." "Thank you" she said, "and what is your name?" "I'm Jeff, Jeff Lynn, Sheriff for Iron County." "Nice to meet you Sheriff. Thank you for coming to our aid today." She said. "You're welcome. I've got to get that power line off the ground and tied up on

that pole so if you'll excuse me." He said.
"Certainly." She replied with a coy look.

The Sheriff returned to the storage unit where he found a ladder but no rope. He carried the ladder down to his truck where he found the rubber gloves and large zip ties he had in his truck for several years, they were meant for crowd control but were never used. He could use them now to secure this power line to the poll. While at the truck he attempted to radio Joe, his deputy at the ski resort, Joe did not answer. He tried Marty as well but got only static. Frustrated he looked to the last of the group leaving in a mini van. He waived them down, it was one of the two smaller men. "Yes Sheriff, what is it?" "I need the power company to come up here and repair this power line, I can't reach anybody on the radio. When you get into town will you report this downed power line to the power company?" "Well certainly Sheriff, do you have their number?" "No I don't but you should be able to look it up once you've got service, it's Iron County CoOp Power and Gas." "Ok sure, we will get it done."

The Sheriff returned to the tree, he set the ladder up on the power pole and walked back to the tree that had the power line pinned under it. He thought to himself, all my life I've been told to never touch a downed power line, and here I am about to touch a downed power line, what? Am I stupid? He put on his rubber gloves, gingerly touched the line with one finger. Nothing. Good he thought, maybe it's dead. He picked it up with one hand, still nothing, he gave it a slight pull, it was stuck under the tree. Just then Bob walked up. "How can I help Sheriff?" "Bring that chain saw down and a shovel if you've got one." "Ok, back in a minute." Looking at the power line, following it up to the pole, he thought, hell, I should just cut it off at the pole and be done with it. Just then Bob returned and ask, "you really think we should be messing with this Sheriff?" "We don't have a choice Bob, these puddles around here, somebody steps in a puddle and the current reaches it, they're dead, we've got to get this off the ground." "Ok Sheriff, I understand, I just think we should wait for the power company." "I don't know when or if they're coming, I asked that guy to call them when he gets into town. We've got to secure it until they get here, we're lucky somebody already hasn't been electrocuted." The Sheriff wrapped both his hands around the wire and pulled, still nothing, it wouldn't budge. "Damn" said the Sheriff, "it must be pinned on a rock." Looking back up at the pole, thinking what he could cut it with, he turned back, grabbed it with both hands, leaned back and pulled with all his weight. The power line was old, it's insulation was brittle and cracked, the slack side of the line fell against the Sheriffs leg and shocked him severely through his pants leg. The Sheriff went stiff and fell back. Bob yelled, "oh God!" Rachel had been watching from above and came running when she saw the Sheriff fall. "Gawd damn!" Yelled the Sheriff! As he sat up! "That will get your attention!" "Oh thank God your alright," said Rachel. "Burnt a hole in my pants but I think I'll survive." "We should leave this for the power company, Sheriff," please, said Bob. "Maybe your right Bob, just wish they'd get here, this is really dangerous."

The smaller man that had told the Sheriff he'd call the power company accelerated his minivan on to the freeway. His daughter said from the passenger seat, "Dad, you told that Sheriff you'd call the power company." "Yes, I'd did, didn't I dear. Can you do it for me, I want to get home before it gets dark." His daughter began to run searches on her cell phone. "What was the name Dad? Pacific Gas and Electric wasn't it?" "No, he said it had iron in it. Iron county or something." She started to type a search when her phone rang, it was her mother. "Thank goodness your safe! Where are you?" "We're in the car on the way home. Why mom, what's the matter?" "Didn't you see the news? I guess you wouldn't up there at camp. There is a tiger loose on that mountain, it's killing people, it killed a University Professor!" "It's not a tiger mom, it's a cougar, that's why we're coming home, the Sheriff closed the camp." "Thank goodness you're on your way. The news said it was a tiger of some kind." "Well mom, the Sheriff said it was a cougar and they chased it thirty miles away but they were closing the camp anyway." "Ok dear, I'm just glad you're safe and on your way home. Let me talk to your father." She handed the phone to her father. "What's going on up there? Why didn't you know about this tiger?" "It's not a tiger dear, it's a cougar." "Oh what's the difference she said, it kills people. Why didn't you know about this?" "Sara was playing music on the radio, with Bluetooth, through her phone, we weren't listening to the news, no one at the camp knew until the Sheriff came." "Ok, well, what time are you going to be home?" "About eight, I think." "Let me talk to Sara." He handed the phone to his daughter. "I love you dear" said the mother, "I love you Mom." "Keep an eye on your Dad, you know he isn't the best driver." "I will mom." With that they hung up and Sara immediately called her friend who she had just left at the camp. "Emily""What?" "Are you still at the camp?" "No, we left, we stopped in Cedar to eat." "Well guess what! It's not a cougar, it's a tiger, that's why they closed the camp. My mom saw it on the news." "A tiger?" "Yes a tiger!" "Wow! No wonder they closed the camp". "Yeah and it ate some Professor." "Wow, wonder if it will eat Marsha?" They both laughed. "I hope so said Sara, she's such a liar and a fake, I hate her." "Me too," said Emily. "She thinks she knows everything because her mom is a teacher." "I know and she thinks Sean likes her but he doesn't." The two girls continued talking as the minivan drove south on I-15.

"Well Bob," said the Sheriff, "if we can't get the power line out from under the tree then we will have to get the tree off the power line. Let's get this saw started." The Sheriff was familiar with this brand and model of saw, he set the choke, placed it on the tree and started pulling the starter, it would not start. He checked the switch, it was on, he continued pulling with Rachel watching about 20 feet off. The saw would not start. "When is the last time this thing ran

Bob?" "I don't know Sheriff, I just got here this week." "Do you have any tools?" "I'll look in the storage unit." The Sheriff walked up past Rachel and said, "nothing is going my way today!" "We're just thankful you're here Sheriff." She replied. He threw the saw on the picnic table next to Bob's smaller saw. "We've got gas in it, let's see if we've got spark." The Sheriff fumbled through the tool box, found the correct socket and removed the spark plug. Pulling the starter cord he saw a good blue spark on the plug. "Well, we've got spark but it's dry, so we're not getting gas. What happens to these Bob, is if they sit for a few months, the gas turns to glue and it plugs up the carb, that's why you have to get non ethanol gas, that won't gum up as fast. There is a little rubber diaphragm in the carburetor that gets glued shut and gas can't get through the carburetor." Bob and Rachel listened intently. As the Sheriff began disassembling the chain saw, they could hear thunder rumbling off in the distance. Great thought the Sheriff, we're going to be here all night. As he took the carburetor apart, Rachel noticed the strands of muscle in his forearms. She said, "it's so nice to have a man around that can do things. My husband can barely change a light bulb." The Sheriff laughed and looked up at Rachel, she was clearly a beautiful woman, she had aged, the stress of her life leaving lines near her eyes, but she was a much sought after woman in her day, the Sheriff could tell. "What does your husband do?" he asked. "He's a tax attorney" she said. "Well, I'd imagine he does very well then wouldn't you say Mrs. Stewart?" "Rachel, call me Rachel Sheriff. Yes, I guess you could say he does well for what he does, she said, with an obvious disdain in her voice." The Sheriff looked at her wedding ring, a three carrot gaudy affair, probably thirty thousand dollars on her finger he thought. She had married for money, for status, both of which she had, but she did not have love or passion in her life and the Sheriff could plainly see that. "There, see that Bob? Rachel? That little rubber diaphragm, it's stuck, glued down with old gas. Now, we will peal it off, clean it up and this saw will fire right up."

Another ten minutes and the Sheriff had started the chain saw. Just as he did ping pong ball sized drops of rain began to fall. Bob yelled over the saw, "don't go down there Sheriff, it's not safe in the rain, with that power line." The Sheriff ignored him and started to walk down toward the tree. Rachel grabbed his arm. "Please don't she said, I don't want to be up here without a capable man." "It will be alright, I've got to get you out of here tonight." He walked down through the driving rain, drove the chain into the tree and started cutting. The chain was very dull, it was very slow and difficult cutting. A puddle was forming at the base of the tree, with the power line in it. He had made one cut through the tree in ten minutes, the puddle was almost at his feet. He pulled the chain saw out in frustration and walked back up the hill where Rachel, Bob and most of the group were waiting under the awning near the fire pit. "I'm sorry folks, things just aren't working out. We're going to have to spend the night here." "What?" Yelled a mother, "we're not spending the night here with a cougar trying to kill us!" The group began talking among themselves. "Look," said the Sheriff, "I don't like it anymore than you do, but you'll be safe, those are steel sleeping quarters, not even a grizzly bear could get into those. You'll be safe in there for the night." "But what about when we need to go to the bathroom," said a younger girl, "they're way over there?" "Bob or I will walk you over, it's not a problem, just relax, we will get through this, the power company should be up here any time and shut that live power line down, until then we can't go near it with the ground wet like that." The rain continued to beat down on the metal roof making it hard for them to talk among themselves. Rachel spoke up. "Let's get ourselves set up in these two sleeping units. Those that want to shower tonight let's get it done before it gets completely dark." The lightening and thunder became very intense, the group moved into the two sleeping units to shelter from the storm. The Sheriff stood under the awning, watching Bob and Rachel assist the group in getting settled in the steel storage units converted into sleeping quarters. After twenty minutes the rain continued to pour, it was nearly dark, Rachel ran out to the awning where the Sheriff was sitting on a picnic table. "What are your plans for the night Sheriff? You are staying with us, right?" "I have to Rachel, it's my job. I'll stay out here on this table, you'll be alright in those sleeping quarters." "No you won't Sheriff, we will make a bed for you in our quarters." "No really, that won't be necessary!" "Oh absolutely it is necessary. Now enough, you're not staying out here tonight." "Ok, well, let me get Bob and see if we can get the generator running." The Sheriff ran through the rain down to Bob's trailer. He banged on the door, Bob opened, squinting out into the darkness and the rain. "We need to get that generator going, where is it?" "Let me get a jacket" Bob said, they both walked up hill briskly in the rain to a cinder block building, Bob unlocked the door with flashlight in hand and they both looked at the generator, which had not ever been started to Bob's knowledge. The Sheriff was familiar with this generator, it was the same brand as one used on the lighted highway emergency signs they used. A Westerbeke, very expensive but also very reliable. The Sheriff checked the oil, fuel, he looked at the battery, it had a separate charging system, he thought, this might just work. He pushed the fuel pump button, he could hear the pump start, he waited, then pushed the starter button, it turned over but did not start. He tried again, still it did not start. He pulled the air cleaner off, put his hand over the intake and pushed the starter again, it fired, again he pushed the starter, the generator started to come to life, at the same time the lights came on in the sleeping units and bathrooms. The girls cheered as the lights came on. "Good" yelled the Sheriff. "I'll be up at the fire pit, we can take turns walking the girls to the bathrooms, I'll take it until midnight, you're on after that, I'll spell you again at two." "Agreed Sheriff." Said Bob.

As the Sheriff walked back to the awning he could see Rachel waiting for him. "Some girls want to shower, can we arrange that." She asked. "Sure" he said. "There are six showers, we should be able to get us all clean inside of a couple hours." She said. "Ok" said the Sheriff, "come get me when the first group is ready to walk over." The showers were about 100 yards from the sleeping units. Three hours later they were all showered and ready for bed. Rachel walked out to the awning and said, "my turn, will you walk with me?" "Certainly" said the Sheriff, who was now getting tired after a long day. At the showers he said, "I'll stand out here until your done." "No" she said, "you stand in that doorway, I don't like being out here alone." "Ok" he said, he stood in the entrance, looking out into the dark, after several minutes he stepped in to rinse his face, he needed to wake up. As he looked up into the mirror he could see Rachel washing her hair, she was indeed a beautiful woman, rinsing the water off her face she opened her eyes and saw him through the mirror. Their eyes met, she was nude, but she did not avert her eyes or move away. He knew it, she knew it, after a moment, he looked away and stepped out through the doorway. A few minutes later she stepped out, fully clothed, took his hand, looked in his eyes and said, "now, walk me back." He did, without saying a word. This capable man was going to get her and her group through this dangerous night. For this night, he was going to be her man.

"Now" she said, "I've fixed you a bunk, this lower one here, right by the door, I'll be in the one across here." "No, really," he said, "I can stay outside," "no you won't, you'll stay in here with us." Several of the teenage girls said yes, we want you here. "Ok" he said, "so it is." He laid on top of the bunk, his service revolver at his side, she turned off the lights and he stared into the darkness. After several minutes he felt her hand on his arm, he reached out and held her hand, which eased their tension and she fell asleep.

It Comes in the Night
Chapter 7

Bob woke up, it was two AM, he had over slept, he knew he had to stand guard for the girls, escort them to the bathrooms. He was groggy, he shook his head, put on his jacket and reached for his flashlight. He stepped out of his trailer, it was dark, foggy, the rain had stopped, he could see mist falling in the lights near the fire pit. He could hear the generator humming in the back ground. He turned on his flashlight and slowly started to walk toward the sleeping units. The generator stopped running, he could hear it wind down, it had run out of gas he thought. He remembered there were gas cans in the storage unit toward the back of the camp area. He slowly walked uphill toward the storage unit. He sensed something, a chill ran down his spine, he looked out into the dark, he saw nothing, he thought of what the Sheriff had said earlier, how it was a cougar but it was 30 miles away. He nervously smiled and continued to walk. He reached the storage unit, inside he found a full five gallon metal gas can. He started to walk back down toward the generator building when again, he felt something watching, he felt terror, he looked out to his left, into the darkness, he could see nothing, but something was there, he dropped the can, turned his light to the darkness, there was a loud hiss, a blast of air, so loud it awoke the Sheriff. In the reflection of the light, Bob saw two slanted eyes above him, then it was quickly on him. Screams rang out into the night, blood curdling screams of a man being torn apart, echoed into the night. The girls awoke in terror, screaming, Rachel flipped the light switch but the lights would not go on. The Sheriff pulled out his flashlight and went for the door. "No" screamed Rachel, "don't leave us alone!" "It's Bob" he yelled, "lock the door, I'll be back." He could hear the women in the other sleeping unit screaming, he ran to where he thought Bob was, he saw nothing, he was pointing his 9mm pistol at nothing. He ran down to Bob's trailer, nothing, he ran back up hill toward the generator building, nothing. His flash light scanning 360 degrees, nothing, nothing but the screaming of the girls and women in the sleeping units. Bob was gone. He ran back to the sleeping unit he came from, he implored Rachel, "please, please calm them down, please, I've got to go to the other unit." "No," screamed several girls, "stay here." "Rochelle" he yelled, "get them under control!" He ran across to the other sleeping unit and pounded on the door, "it's me, the Sheriff open up!" One of the mothers opened the door, sobbing irrationally. He hugged her, "it's going to be alright, it's going to be alright." The girls and women were crying, "please, calm them down, I'll get the lights back on." "What happened Sheriff?" Yelled one of the mothers, "I don't know" he said, "I don't know, just keep the door locked and stay inside." He ran back to the generator room, threw open the door, he checked the fuel tank, it was empty. He looked outside, toward the storage unit, his flash light illuminated a red steel gas can laying on the ground, it's lid dripping gas. He walked up to it realizing, this was where Bob was when the attack occurred. He picked up the gas can, used his flash light to scan the area, fifty yards off in the trees he saw something he did not want to see, what he knew, were Bob's remains. It was Bob's upper torso, his head and one shoulder and arm still attached. "My God" he said, a wave a nausea swept over him. He turned back, took the gas can to the generator room, filled the tank and started the generator. He walked back to the sleeping units, Rachel let him in, the lights were on, several girls were crying while others held them. One mother stood up and walked to the "Sheriff, you're going to get us out of here, right now! We can't take this any more!" "You're safe, you're safe in here, just wait until morning, when the sun comes up we will get some help." He walked back to the door, Rachel took his arm, "we're going to be alright aren't we Sheriff, you're going to get us out of here aren't you?" "Yes, we will make it, I promise you, we will make it out of here, just try to calm the girls." The Sheriff walked over to the other sleeping unit, consoling the women there, he stepped back out into the darkness, he knew he had to do something with the remains of Bob, before morning light and the girls saw the horror he had just seen. He looked out into the darkness, wondered what was out there, was it still out there? He took a deep breath, checked his 9mm and started out into the woods where he had seen the remains. Bob's eyes were wide open, the blank stare of absolute terror upon his face, the Sheriff looked away. He reached down and grabbed Bob's remaining hand and began to drag his torso back to camp. As he did there was a deep growl that came out of the woods. The Sheriff froze in his tracks, he looked out into the darkness, he raised his flashlight to his left, there in the trees he saw those slanted eyes, the same eyes he had seen in the darkness of the lava tube cave, he raised his 9mm and fired off four rounds into those eyes, the girls screamed as the Sheriff could hear the beast moving fast through the trees, he could not see it, but it was moving fast and away. Grabbing Bob's hand he dragged the remains as fast as he could toward Bob's trailer. He saw Rachel step out of the sleeping unit and repulse back at the sight of the Sheriff dragging Bob's half body across the camp. He dragged the remains into Bob's trailer, closed the door and looked back to the sleeping units. He had a hundred yards to run uphill to get back to the safety of the sleeping units. One deep breath and he sprinted uphill and got to the door, he pounded but it wasn't opened, he yelled "Rachel, let me in!" She slowing opened the door, he had blood on his hand, she recoiled back and starred at him. He looked at her, "don't say a word." She shook her head, "no, I won't." "God what was that?" "Don't!" He said, "I'll explain later," he looked up, the girls were crowded to the back of the sleeping unit. "We're going to be alright" he said, "the suns coming up in a few hours, we're going to be alright. Nothing can get us inside these steel buildings, we're going to be alright!" "We're not going to be alright" a 17 year old screamed, "that thing is going to kill us! Kill us! You lied! You lied to us!" He looked at Rachel and said, "Go! Calm them down." Just then lightening and thunder cracked over head, the rain started. The Sheriff stepped out, rinsing the blood off his hand in the rain, he ran to the other sleeping unit, inside he saw the women and children crowded in the back. "It's going to be alright" he said, "we're going to get out of here! You're safe in this steel building, it will be light soon, we're going to get out of here!" One of the mothers asked, "was that Bob? Where is Bob?" The Sheriff looked at the floor and paused, I can't lie to them he thought. "Bob's gone, there's nothing we can do for Bob, let's just keep calm, the sun will come up and we will get out of here." Some started crying, he looked to one of the older women, motioned for her to come to him, she did. "What's your name" he asked. "Cheryl" she replied. "Cheryl I need you to take charge here, keep things calm, panic and fear won't help. The sun will come up and we will get out of here." "Ok Sheriff, I'll do the best I can but we are scared, terrified!" "I know you are but we're going to be fine, nothing can get through these steel walls, we are safe!" He started counting people, too many to fit in the bed of his truck, I've got to clear that tree he thought. Two more hours, the sun will be up, two more hours.

Outside in the rain, he scanned the area with his flash light, nothing. He ran back to the other unit and called for Rachel. She opened the door and let him in, he sat on the bunk, she stood looking at him. "Now what she asked?" "We wait until sun up, we wait." "Where is it" she asked? "Did you kill it?" "I don't know, I just don't know. No, it ran, I don't think it's dead, I got off four rounds but I don't think it's dead." She sat down on the bunk next to him, she took his hand, her hand was cold, ice cold he thought, and shaking. He looked at her, "you've got to calm down, we can't panic." "Can't panic," she asked? "What we're you doing out there? Was that, that, that part of Bob that you were dragging?" "I couldn't leave his remains out there, you shouldn't have seen that." "Shouldn't have? Well I did! And I can't unsee it!" She said. "And we can't have anyone else see that so I had to lock it in his trailer! I had to!" He said. She grabbed his face and pulled hers next to his, she broke down crying, "oh god" she said, "hold me, hold me." He laid back in his bunk, she laid next to him, put her leg over his. She clung tight to him with her head on his chest. He looked up at one of the other women, she seemed to understand. He looked down at her blonde hair, he felt her tears soak through his shirt, two hours he thought, two hours.

The time dragged on, the rain continued to beat down, Rachel was practically on top of him, his watch read 5:40am, the sun should be coming up. He moved, asked Rachel to let him up, "no, please, just stay here, stay here until someone comes for us." She looked up and kissed him on the mouth, pressed her hand into his chest. He pulled her closer as a husband would a wife, comforting her. He looked up at the others, some were asleep, some were starring at the floor. He looked back down at her, felt the warmth of her body next to his. He didn't want to go out there, in the cold rain, but he knew he had to. He sat up, she put her hand on top of his thigh and looked into his eyes. "Please" he said, "I've got to get us out of here." "No, you don't, you don't, let's just wait." "We can't, there is no one coming, the power company should have been here by now, they're not, so I've got to get us out of here." "Please" she said, sliding her hand on to his stomach. "No, I've got to move that tree." He stood up, looked down at her, "I've got to go." Some of the others looked up at him, he stepped out the door, it was cold, but it was getting light, the rain continued but it was lighter now. He placed a fresh clip in his 9mm, walked down toward the tree, he could see there was about 3 inches of standing water around the tree, he knew the power line was under that water. Shit he thought, I've got to keep people away, but how? This was right at the entrance to the camp, drivers would turn in and be right at the tree, anyone stepping out of their car would step right into that puddle and get electrocuted. He looked at his truck, parked about 50 yards back from the entrance, if he could pull his truck into the entrance, that would block anyone from coming in and driving into that puddle. He would have to hike to the south, climb the fence, get on the road and drive his truck into the entrance then hike back around. But what about the cat, the mountain lion, was it still out there? He needed a back up plan, if he didn't make it, a way to get these women and kids out of here, if he didn't make it.

He walked back up to the sleeping unit, Rachel let him in. "Listen" he said, "we need to talk." She looked at him, "so talk," she said. He looked up, the others were listening, "not here" he said, "not here." "Where then" she said, "out side" he said. "I'm not going out there!" "It will be alright, it's almost light." She followed him out, he looked over at the showers, "over there" he said. They ran through the light rain, to the showers. Once inside, she looked into his eyes, he said "we need a back up plan, a way for you to get out of here if I don't make it."   She shook her head, said "no," she put her finger over his lips, pulled him close and kissed him passionately. "You, are not going anywhere!" She said. He pulled her hard into him, she could feel his body rise, she pulled at his shirt, he pulled hers over her head. They began making love, making love with an animalistic intensity, the stress and emotions of the situation released by their passion. It was violent, rough, a release of all their fears. The anxiety and stress of both of their lives freed from them in this one moment of passion. She lay on the counter, gasping for air, he stepped back, then started again. All of their existence was focused in this moment, they were consumed, there was nothing else. Breathing heavily, he stepped back again and said, "god we can't do this," she said, "shut up, I want you." He returned, again and again, then stepped back, around into the shower, hanging one hand on the shower head, gasping heavily, he turned on the shower. A few moments later she entered the shower, climbing on him they continued until both were exhausted. He let her down, pushed her against the wall and began again, it was as if all the frustrations of his life and all of her life were being satisfied in this one moment, neither wanted it to end. They held each other in the stream of the shower. Stepping out, gasping for air while toweling off, she looked at him and said, "Now, what is your plan." He looked at her knowing, his life was forever altered.

An Altered Reality

Chapter 8

Christine awoke to find her bed empty, her husband not there. This was not the first time her husband had worked all night, but it was the first time he was dealing with an emergency that drew national attention. A primitive lion roaming the mountains of Iron County killing people, according to the media. She showered and prepared for the day. She drove to the Sheriff's office and walked in the door where Marty sat at her desk. "Where is Jeff" she asked? Marty hesitated, immediately suspecting she was being accused of doing something inappropriate with her boss, Christine's husband. She was obviously flustered which made Christine suspect something was going on with this 32 year old divorcée who spent too much time with her husband. Marty finally responded. "I don't know" she said! Christine found this hard to believe, knowing the routine of the office. "You haven't spoken to him on the radio?" "Not since yesterday, he was going up to close the girls camp." Christine's anger was nearing a boiling point but what Marty said rang true, she knew he was going up there, her emotions started to cool. "That's it? That's all you know?" "Yes Mrs. Lynn, that's all I know." Christine starred at Marty, Marty's eyes could not meet Christine's, knowing how she wanted Christine's husband, how she had touched him the day before. Christine knew something was up, but she also knew her husband had told her he had to close the girls camp. And she knew what happened in the cave the day before. "I'm going up there" she said. "No, wait" said Marty, "let me radio Joe, they were supposed to meet yesterday at the ski resort. Base to four," "Four go ahead." "Joe have you seen the Sheriff?" She asked. "No." He replied. "Do you know where he is?" She asked. "He was at the girls camp, he was going to meet me at the ski resort but he never showed up. We were on the radio but there was too much static I couldn't understand him." He replied. "Where are you now Joe?" She asked. "I'm on my way to a doctors appointment with my wife." "10-4 base out." Marty looked up at Christine, "his wife's got cancer." "I know," Christine said. It was a sobering comment for both women whose emotions were running high. "Let me call the camp," Marty said. The phone rang busy. "That phone has been busy for two days." Christine walked to the door, looked out the window. "Something has happened, I can feel it."

While standing there, a pickup truck pulled into the parking lot. It was Donald Brown. He walked in and asked, "where's the Sheriff?" "We'd all like to know that" said Christine. "Hi, I'm Christine, Jeff is my husband." "He was at the girls camp the last anyone heard," said Marty. Donald shook his head, "you know we tracked that cat right through that camp." "What!" Christine said! "Oh I'm sorry, that's right, I'm not supposed to say anything." "Say anything? Say anything about what?" "I'm not sure I should say." "Look at me! That's my husband out there, you're damn well going to say!" "Yes Ma'am, yes Mrs. Lynn. We were attacked, two days ago, in a cave in the lava fields east of Radar Peak." "What do you mean attacked?" "We went in the cave tracking my dogs GPS. The Professor froze and the lion killed him." "Did you see it?"She asked. "No, well, no, I saw it's eyes, in the dark, but nothing else." "Then how do you know it killed the Professor." "Because I heard it! And I saw it's eyes, it was right on him." "How do you know it's a cat," she asked. "Well, I hunt cougars for a living, that's what I do, I'm a guide. My dogs hit on the scent of a cougar when we started tracking. That and the eyes, it's got a cats eyes, slanted and yellow green. Only, this is different." "Different how," asked Christine. "It's big, Mrs. Lynn, really big. A big cat, a Tom cougar, will weigh 150-180 pounds and it's about waist high to me and I'm six foot. But this things eyes were above mine, so it has to be six foot at the shoulders." "My god" said Christine. "And the tracks, they were bigger around than dinner plates, and spread four feet apart, that's four feet at the hip." Marty starred off into space as if in shock. "And my husband is out there with this thing? Why didn't you tell anyone?" "Because he ordered me not to Mrs. Lynn!" "Good god! Marty, can we get any help from the state? The state patrol or another county?" She asked. "I can try Mrs. Lynn, I'm not sure who to call, I just started here six months ago." Marty said. "Call Salt Lake County" said Donald, "it was their helicopter that flew us up there." "Yes, Salt Lake, call them Marty. I'm going to call the Department of Wild Life, they should be tracking this animal not my husband." The two women started working the phones. At the same time multiple calls were coming in from people concerned about loved ones on the mountain. Donald left, headed to his friends house to see if he could use his dogs to start another hunt.

Back at the girls camp, the Sheriff and Rachel walked back into the sleeping unit. They had been gone an hour. Two of the women knew immediately what had happened in the showers, they could read it on their faces, the way they walked and now moved, as a couple. Some of the women were disgusted and beyond angry but could not express it in front of the girls, several of which were still trembling in fear over the horrific events of the night. "We have to discuss our plans for leaving the camp," the Sheriff said. "I need the group together at the fire pit." One of the girls said "no, we're not going out there!" The group agreed. "No way" said one mother, "no way we're going out there with that thing, whatever it is." He looked at them, looked down at the floor and said, "It's safe, it's safe, it's day light now, it only comes out at night," One mother replied. "And you lied to us before Sheriff, about us getting out of here, we don't trust you anymore!" The Sheriff shook his hard and said, "You're going to have to trust me ladies, it's the only way we're going to get out of here."

Just then the sound of a horn honking came from the entrance. "No!" said the Sheriff as he turned to run out the door. It was a mini van, the father of one of the girls had seen the news about the lion and drove up to get his daughter and wife. The van was pulled up to the tree, it's wheels in three inches of water, the Sheriff began to run toward the van. As he did some of the girls and women from the other sleeping unit came out to see who it was. Just then the man opened the drivers door and the Sheriff yelled, "no!" As he ran toward the van. The man was distracted by the sight of the Sheriff running and yelling, he stepped out to hear what he was saying. His body stiffened like a board and fell face first into the water, electrocuted as his wife and daughter watched in horror. The Sheriff stopped, stunned by the sight, he heard the wife scream as she ran toward her husband. He turned and saw her headed for the same fate, he sprinted meeting her ten yards before the water, tackling her at full speed as the daughter watched in stunned silence, not understanding what was happening to her parents. She started to stumble toward her mother who was on the ground screaming as she was held down by the Sheriff. Rachel saw this and ran to the girl, hugging her, turning her away from the awful scene. The girl crying, "no, no, my mom, my dad, no, no, make them stop, no." Others ran toward them, the Sheriff holding one arm up while he held the woman down, "No! Stop! Go back" he yelled. They stopped, confused by what they were seeing. He yelled again, "go back! Get back." Rachel walked the sobbing girl over to Cheryl and asked her, "please, take her." She then turned and ran down to the Sheriff, past the group standing 20 feet back. She knelt down and helped him lift the hysterical woman to her feet. Both holding her they walked her up the hill. The woman trying to turn back and get to her husband who was dead, electrocuted face down in the water.

Loss of Control
Chapter 9

After witnessing the death of the man at the entrance to the camp, the group was starting to lose control. They were exhausted from being up all night, exhausted from the constant fear and exhausted from trying to hold back their emotions. The yelling and screaming was drowning out the Sheriffs attempt to calm the group. Girls were crying and running back to the sleeping units, crawling under the bunks, several women were yelling at the Sheriff, "you've got to get us out of here, I can't take this any more, get us out of here! Now!" Yelled one mother.

Unable to reason or yell above the screaming women, the Sheriff turned in frustration and looked down the hill, at the van and the dead man in the water. He looked at the power pole and the aluminum ladder leaning against it and said, "fuck it!" He would have to risk it before absolute chaos broke out and more people died. He walked over to the storage unit and flipped on the light, looking through the tools hanging on the wall, he found a pair of branch cutters. Looking along the wall, he saw several pairs of rubber muck boots. He went through them looking for a size he could wear, one with out holes. The only ones he could put on had a tear in the side. Damn he thought. He looked in the tool box, there behind it a roll of duct tape. He taped over the tear in the side of the boots then put them on, wrapping additional layers over the torn area. He walked out toward the table and his rubber gloves lay next to the chain saw he had repairs. He put the gloves on, they were damp inside, he didn't know if that mattered but he had to press on. Rachel looked toward him, saw the rubber boots, the cutters and knew immediately what he was going to do. She ran across the camp toward him. "No" she yelled! "No! Don't do it." He ignored her and walked toward the power pole. "No, stop" she cried as she reached him, "I love you!" He stopped, looked her in the eyes and said, "I have to, someone else will die if I don't." "You will die if you do" she yelled back. "I have to take that chance." "No! No you don't! Please stop! I love you!" He took a deep breath and looked at her and said, "then let me do what I have to do." He continued walking to the power pole. "No," she said crying, "Oh God please don't, I need you, I've been alone for so long, please no, please don't." He stopped again and turned to her, look, he said, "I'm not planning on dying, but I've got to cut that line or someone else will die." She continued to plead with him, but she saw the look in his eyes and knew, she could not stop him. He continued to the pole.

At the standing waters edge, he looked at the dead man, there was no movement. He glanced down in the water, he could see dead worms, stiff in the electrical current. The aluminum ladder stood in the water, as did the wood power pole. He walked carefully around the edge of the water to the closest edge to the power pole. He reached down and pressed the tape against his boot again. He took a breath and stepped into the water. Nothing, he felt nothing. He slowly walked three steps to the ladder, using one hand he placed it on the ladder with his wet rubber glove, again, nothing, he was, so far, insulated from the electrical current. Holding the cutters in his left hand he started to climb the ladder, being careful not to touch it with anything but his rubber boots and gloves. Climbing he focused all of his attention on the ladder, his boots and gloves, he looked nowhere else. Rachel stood 50 feet off with her hands covering her mouth, watching in horror. He reached the top of the ladder, he knew he was just below the wire now. He looked up and started to lose his balance, swinging wildly with his hand holding the cutters, he reached around the pole and saved himself from falling into the electrified water below. Regaining his composure, he worked to establish his balance with his feet, releasing the pole and ladder with his hands, he gripped the plastic grips on the steel tree branch cutters. Slowing moving his eyes up he began to raise the cutters to the wire. Again, he lost his balance and nearly fell to his death. Breathing heavily, he felt himself growing weak, losing his composure, he fought hard to control his fear, his anxiety. He thought, ok, I can hold on with one hand, put the cutters on the wire with the other, then quickly grab them with my other and cut the wire. Putting the cutters in his right hand, holding on with his left, he looked up and put the cutters on the wire. There, he froze, and held position. Now he must let go of the pole with his left hand, grab the left cutter handle and cut the wire. Would the tree trimmers cut through the wire? If they didn't and he fell, he would be electrocuted. He looked at the cutters, they looked new, as if they had never been used. He thought of his father, and all of the things they had done together, when he was a boy, how strong and brave his father had been, even when dying with cancer. He took a breath, released his hand from the pole, grabbed the handle of the cutter and with all his strength brought the handles together. This threw his weight to the right which caused the ladder to shift to the left, he was falling. Rachel screamed out in terror, as did the other women watching further up the hill. He knew his life depended on cutting that wire and all of his focus, was upon squeezing those two handles together. He fell ten feet into the cold shallow water below, landing back first with his arms extended upward clamping the tree branch cutters together.

Had he cut the wire? Was his first thought? He sudden realized, he was alive, he must have! Kicking to get himself up he looked at the cutters with the severed power line still in them, the hot wire now twelve feet up on the pole. "Thank God" he said knelling in the water, "thank you God, thank you Dad." Rachel ran through the puddle and began kissing his cheek, "Oh thank you, thank you, thank you God." He rose to his feet. "Now" he said, "we have to clear this tree." Turning, he saw the body of the dead man, still face down in the water. He looked at Rachel and asked, "can you get me something to cover him with?" She ran up hill to the sleeping unit to get a blanket. Reaching down, the Sheriff rolled the dead man over, looking at his face, this was a good man he thought, a loving man, a man who loved his family. He pulled him by his arms off into the trees, placing the blanket that Rachel brought over him. He felt immense frustration, that this man had died because he did not get that power line cut, the day before. He fought back those feelings, knowing he had thirty women and children he had to get off the mountain before night fall.

Walking up the hill toward the chain saw, Rachel held on to his arm. Behind them came the sound of a car arriving on the gravel road. He turned to look and it was Christine , his wife, in her SUV. She looked up the hill and saw her husband, with a blonde woman clinging to his arm. He turned to Rachel and said, it's

my wife. Rachel froze in her tracks, suddenly
realizing the reality of the situation, the man she was
clinging to was married and his wife was here.
Christine stepped out of her SUV, parked on the road
and began walking toward her husband. He started
walking toward her, they met at the tree, she kissed
him and said "thank God you're safe." Who is that
woman? "Rachel, she is the camp leader, we've had
a terrible time, two dead, you've got to help me get
these people out of here." "Ok" she said, "what do
you need?" "I met your tracker Donald, he's bringing
more dogs." "Good" he said, "I need you to gather
these women, have them get their things and start
loading their cars, they will be afraid of the lion
coming back but you have to get them in their cars.
Rachel will help you." Christine paused, "have you
seen the lion?" "Yes, I saw it last night, I shot it, I
hope it's dead but I don't know. It only comes out at
night dear, it only comes out at night, please, get
them in their cars." Christine nodded her head,
looked uphill at Rachel and walked toward her. The
Sheriff did not know what Rachel would say or what
his wife would say, but he also knew his wife would
know, she would sense it and he would have to tell
her the truth.

He drove the chain saw deep into the tree, he cut the tree into ten foot lengths, sections that he could drag off the road with his truck. He did not stop, the chain throwing water back on him, he was soaked and cold but he cut until the job was done. Glancing up he saw groups of women and girls with suit cases and bags at the top of the hill, waiting to come to their cars. He saw his wife, talking face to face with Rachel, he knew his life was yet in jeopardy, not his physical life but his life with the woman he had loved for nearly thirty years. But he would not stop, focused on the large tree, the work was a way to delay what he knew was coming. Hooking a nylon strap under the tree sections, laying in the water to get it done, he dragged the strap back to his truck pulling the ten foot logs off the road. With the women watching from above he stood in the puddle on the road, looking to his left he saw the body of the man who had been electrocuted in the puddle, and the phone wires still laying in the ground. Walking up the hill, soaking wet he stood before the group, "now, let's get you in your cars and on your way home!" A quiet cheer went up from the group. He looked to his left, his wife starring at him with a stern look. "Christine," he said, "will you take the names of each person and phone numbers before walking them to their cars." Without hesitation she got out her cell phone and started making the list. Rachel approached the Sheriff, he held his hand up and said, "please, not now, not here." He walked the first group down to their cars, his hand near his 9mm pistol with eyes scanning the surrounding trees for any movement. He asked the three women driving, please be careful, there has been a lot of rain, the roads will be slick. With that they drove their cars through the puddle and past the body of the man who had died there. After all those who had stood outside the sleeping units had left, Christine said, "there are five more in the back of that unit who will not come out, they are terrified, shaking with fear." He said, "two of those are the wife and daughter of the dead man, we have to move him out of sight before we take them out. We need medical assistance with these others, they may need sedation before we move them." Looking back down the hill, he saw the phone wires and thought, if he could get them reconnected he could call ambulances to take the body and help the others leave the mountain. But he also knew that exposed power line was up on that pole as well. He knew he had to take the chance, otherwise they'd be up here for another night.

With his knife he stripped the phone wires on the ground so he could reconnect them to those still on the pole. He felt the sting of the low voltage in the hot wire, as he stood soaking wet in the water. Looking up on the pole he saw the phone wires on the opposite side of the pole from the exposed end of the power line he had cut earlier in the day. Tying the phone wire to his belt loop he climbed the ladder, quickly this time with both hands on the ladder. Using the knife, he stripped the phone wires on the pole so he could tie them back together with the wires attached to those on his belt loop. The power line 18 inches from the phone lines, he stopped and looked at it, it was death, no less than that lion out there, no less than a bullet in the forehead, it was death and it was right there, inches away. He looked up the hill, his wife and Rachel standing next to each other watching as he stood atop the ladder. Pulling the phone wire from his belt loop, he twisted the wires together, mindful to avoid the power line, backing down the ladder he yelled above to Christine, "see if the phone works! If it does call Mercy Ambulance and tell them we got two fatalities and six transports that need sedation." Christine started to look for where the phone might be, she checked the sleeping units then walked down to Bob's trailer. Just as she opened the door the Sheriff saw her and yelled "no!" She screamed in horror and recoiled back, falling to the dirt, having seen the torso of Bob, on the floor of the trailer with heart and entrails still attached. The Sheriff ran to her, her face in her hands sobbing. "What did you do!" she screamed? "What did you do? Why? What did you do?" He tried to console her but she rose to her feet. "Get away from me, don't touch me!" He stepped back. She looked at Rachel, looked at him, turned and walked to her SUV. He started to walk down to her, she screamed at him, "get away!" She started the vehicle and drove off. He turned up and looked at Rachel, she looked down and walked away. He stood there, knowing, regardless of the outcome, his life would never be the same. He walked toward the storage shed, his mind gone blank, starring off into the distance, feeling as though he might throw up.

The sound of a phone ringing shook him from his stupor. In the generator room, the phone was ringing. He walked over and picked it up. It was Marty, reaching for the generator shut down switch, he killed the generator. "Marty" he said, "yes Sheriff," "I need you to call mercy ambulance, have them send three units, we've got two fatalities and six that possibility need sedation and transport." "Yes Sheriff I will but," he interrupted her and said, "get the power company up here, tell them it's a downed line, an emergency, get them up here as soon as possible." "Yes Sheriff but," "but what Marty," he said. "Are you alright" she asked, in her most feminine voice. "No, he said, no, I'm a damn long way from alright Marty." She asked, "when will I see you again," "I don't know Marty, I don't know." With that he hung up. Walking back toward the fire pit, avoiding Rachel and the others, he sat down on a bench, then he laid down, closing his eyes, he had not slept in the past two days.

The sounds of sirens echoed up the canyon as the ambulances approached the girls camp. The Sheriff sat up, blinking his eyes as the EMTs walked up the hill toward him. "What do we have Sheriff," said the lead driver. "Two women four girls in the steel building to the right. Two of them watched their father, their husband, die this morning, electrocuted. His body is at the base of the hill just behind that power pole. You need to get him in the ambulance now. You've got human remains in the trailer, gruesome remains. They need to be bagged and preserved for evidence. The girls, the women are traumatized, you may need sedatives." "Ok Sheriff" he said, "and you?" "I'll be fine, let's just get this cleaned up so we can get out of here."

Two trucks pulled up below, he recognized Donald Brown stepping out of one, the other with a horse trailer behind. He shook his head, not now, I can't do this now. Donald walked up the hill briskly. "What's happened? What's going on up here Sheriff?" He yelled. "Not now Donald, I can't do this now Donald, I'm exhausted, I need to go home." He said. "Was it here Sheriff?" Asked Donald. The Sheriff looked up, disappointed in Donald's persistence, "yes, it killed the camp counselor." "Did you see it," Donald asked? "I saw it's eyes, in the dark, I shot it, four rounds, I shot it, I heard it run off." Donald excitedly replied. "We've got horses and dogs Sheriff, we're going to track that son of a bitch and kill it." "Not now Donald, I can't." The Sheriff replied in an exhausted voice. "You don't need to Sheriff, we'll handle it." "No, no you're not. The sheriff said sternly. I'm not dealing with more dead people, Donald!" "Well, you can't stop us Sheriff, I know the law, under the law this is vermin that is putting life and property at risk, we're hunting it down and we're killing it, and you can't stop us." Yelled Donald. The Sheriff stood up, looked Donald in the eye, then turned to see the EMTs loading the body into the ambulance below. Knowing he couldn't leave until the women and girls were transported off the mountain, he told Donald, "Do what you will."

Walking back to the sleeping unit, he could hear girls crying, stepping in, Rachel rose and wrapped her arms around him. "I'm so sorry, so sorry, I didn't mean to," he interrupted her, "mean to do what?" She took his arm and led him out the door. "I didn't say anything, she just knew," she said, "she could tell." "I know" said the Sheriff, "she's always been that way, she knows, she senses things." "Will I ever see you again?" She asked. "You've got a husband" he said. "I'm leaving him, this has changed my life, I'm not living that life anymore, it's not worth it, I want a real life now, real love." She looked in his eyes. "I can't he said, I don't know what's going to happen, it's just best that we part for now, I love my wife. I can't believe this is where I'm at, please he said, let me go, let me finish this, we will deal with the rest later." She looked in his eyes, he would not look at her, she wanted to kiss him but could see he was spent, exhausted in every sense of the word. She stepped back, looked at him, turned and walked back in the door.

Looking down the hill, the Sheriff saw Donald release the hounds, mounting the horses as the hounds raced straight up through the camp and to the west, Donald stopped his horse at the Sheriff, "we're going to get it Sheriff, we're not stopping until we do." Just then, the sounds of the dogs changed, as if they had stopped and had the prey cornered. Donald kicked his horse and was off at a full run to the west, pulling his rifle out as he left. The Sheriff turned and began to walk toward the baying hounds, which sounded as if they were only 100 yards off. Walking upon the scene, two horses and four hounds and two men surrounding a large dead animal, Donald turned and yelled, "you killed it Sheriff, it's dead, you killed it!" The Sheriff walked up with a troubled look on his face and said, "What the hell is that beast? My god, where did that thing come from?" Donald replied. "I don't know Sheriff, I've never seen anything like it, it's as big as a horse! Look at the size of that damn thing!" The men walked to its head, look at the fangs on that cat! Foot long fangs protruded from the mouth of a huge dead lion, bigger than any of them had ever seen. The sheriff kneeled down at its head and said, "this is what the Professor said it was, a Saber Tooth Tiger. How the hell it got here we may never know. We've got to get the University people up here, this makes no sense, how something like this could even be up here, how can it even exist." "Look at that Sheriff, you nailed that son of a bitch, right in the eyes." He turned to Donald, "keep the hounds off it, we've got to get it tested, there might be more of these, this is beyond anything I've ever seen, beyond all else Donald, beyond all else, these cats were supposed to be extinct ten thousand years ago, I can't believe what we're looking at. Get those hounds back in the truck, we've got to secure the area."

Walking back toward the camp, the sheriff saw the EMTs leading the women and girls down toward the ambulance. He walked into the generator room, picked up the phone and called Marty. "Marty?" "Yes! She said. Thank god you're safe Sheriff, thank you for calling me back!" "Listen Marty, I need you to get those University people back up here again he said, at the girls camp. I don't think they're going to come Sheriff, I spoke with the chairman over there, he said he is pretty upset with you getting their Professor killed," said Marty. "He was some kind of big shot." "Tell them we've got it Marty, tell them we killed it, we've got their lion. Tell them to get up here and get it." He said. "Ok I will Sheriff, that's so exciting you killed it!" She said. "Call that forensic team out of Salt Lake as well, get them up here ASAP." He said. "You've got it Sheriff, when will you be back" she asked. "I going home Marty, I haven't slept in two days. I'll have Donald lead these people to the cat but I have to go home and get some sleep." "Ok Sheriff, I understand, don't worry about a thing, I'll handle it, get some rest." With that he hung up the phone, turned to walk out and there stood Rachel, now alone, she pulled him to her, she kissed him deeply. She looked at him and didn't say a word. He looked down at the ground, turned and walked away, sick inside, knowing his wife was not coming back.

"And Because of Iniquity"

Chapter 10

Her SUV was not in the garage as he pulled his truck in. He knew she wouldn't be home. Looking at the kitchen table, there was no note, nothing. Walking in the bedroom, he sat on the bed, kicked his boots off, took off his belt and laid back, looking at the ceiling he thought, it just got out of control, out of control, so much, so fast. How did he let it get so out of control? Why? Why did it all come unraveled so fast? His mind raced, he was exhausted to the point that he could not sleep, but he did sleep, he fell hard asleep, troubled by what had transpired in the previous days and what had become of his life. He was approaching 60 hours with no sleep, he collapsed. He slept for twelve hours and awoke to an empty house, bewildered at his now altered existence. It was 4:00am and he had never felt so alone. Looking in the garage, her car was still not there, he walked back in, stared at the living room he had shared with his wife for nearly 30 years. He walked back into the bedroom, fell face down on the bed, he wanted to cry, he felt the emotion but he could not, he was stiff, he was cold, his face felt hard.

He left for work early, drove around town, not sure what he was looking for, he knew where his wife was, at her sisters, but he didn't want to go there, he didn't know what he would say. Stepping into his office, Marty was at her desk. She could sense he was troubled, deeply troubled, she did not press the matter, knowing the limitations of her relationship with him. "The university people and the crimes unit will be on the mountain today," she said. "Good" he said, looking at her for the first time. "The Salt Lake County Sheriffs office wants you to call them, they want to know about the Professor, they want to retrieve his body." He shook his head, "I don't know if there is a body Marty." She winced at the statement and said. "Well, they want to talk to you Sheriff." He looked at the floor and said. "I don't want to talk to them. Just set it up, have them fly down, I'll meet them at the airport and lead them to the cave." "Ok Sheriff," she said.

He walked into his office and closed the door. Starring at his computer, looking at the stack of accumulated mail, none of it he wanted to deal with, he felt trapped, trapped in a thick tar and sinking. He saw no way to fix what he had done, what he had failed to do and the pain that caused others, innocent people who deserved none of this. His wife, the family of the electrocuted man, Bob's family, the Professor. The enormity of the past few days washed over him like a wave of black oil. He could not avoid responsibility, he must accept it, accept it all, it was his and he knew it, he took on the mantle of Sheriff, of Husband and protector of those who needed protection. In his mind, he had failed on all counts, he could not live with it.

After an hour he got up, there was no resolution, his wife was right to leave him, he had violated the most sacred thing in his life, his marriage. She would not forgive him, he would not further disrespect her by asking. He was so angry, so angry with himself, livid, he had failed in the worst way. The Professor, a horrid death because of him. And that poor man, that good man, that so needlessly died, electrocuted while his family watched! And why? Why? Because he didn't secure that power line when he had a chance? The man was dead, because of him. And Rachel, what the hell was he thinking? These are unforgivable, it was as if he threw his entire life away in the last few days. It was as if everything he had worked for, in his life was now nothing, trash buried under his inability to handle the events of the last few days. How did it get to here? Where did he lose control? How?

The exhaustion of the previous week had worn him down and now he was guilty of things he had never before imagined, he could or would have done. Locked in the grip of a deep depression that was taking hold of him, he got up from his desk and walked out the front door, ignoring Marty's inquiries, he stepped in his patrol truck and drove off. He did not know where he was going or why, just somewhere, anywhere but here. On the freeway, he drove north for twenty minutes, his thoughts locked on what he had done, the darkness pressing down on him like a heavy weight, the sorrow turned to rage and he pushed the accelerator pedal to the floor. The truck built for police duty, accelerated to over 130 mph.

Christine sat at the breakfast table with her sister. To break the uncomfortable silence, her sister asked, "what are you going to do?" Christine continued to stare at her cup of coffee. Her sister got up and walked into the kitchen. Christine was locked in a cross fire of emotions, rage, sorrow, grief, bewilderment and disbelief. She knew what had happened the moment she looked in that woman's eyes, but it was as if she went into denial, carried on as if, because as if, was the only thing she could do with the tidal wave of emotion that hit her. Her husband, unfaithful? That was simply not a possibility, her mind reasoned, yet in her heart she knew he had been with that woman, she knew it the moment she looked in her eyes. Then that grotesque torso in the trailer, what was left of that man, the shock brought her restraint to a collapse, she could constrain herself no further. She had to leave that camp and the closest person in her life, the man she loved who had betrayed her.

And now what? What remains? What does she want to remain? Suddenly she was alone in a strange world, where betrayal had made her intimate companion, her lover, the love of her life, now her hated enemy. It was a bizarre twisted world she had never before known. His betrayal, that foul act, had made him a stranger, a murderer who killed the most sacred thing in her life, the love she had for him. He was now the most intense enemy she had ever known but at the same time, the man she loved! It was impossible.

There was no one now, not her sister, not her Bishop, no one else left in this world. It was as if they were all strangers to her, speaking words that were meaningless, because they could never understand. She was alone, she knew no one, there was not anyone that understood the world she now lived in, she was a stranger in a bizarre and foreign place.

Betrayal, betrayal at the deepest level had done this and there was no changing it.

She got up from the table, walked into the bedroom and collapsed to her knees, laying her face on the bed she sobbed heavily, the emotion was coming out now and she could not stop it. The one person, closest to her in this world, the one she trusted without question, violated her, drove the knife in and killed her heart. This adultery had left her raped, gutted, irreparably torn from any sense of normality. She was drowning in a river of darkness, yet she would not die. Consumed in rage and revenge but against who? The only man she had ever loved? She faced this terrible question alone now in an irrational dangerous universe. Should she fight to live or lay down and die. What in God's name had happened and why? How did her world change so violently, so fast. One moment she was concerned for her husbands safety, the next he has violated and disgraced all she ever held sacred. Why? She did not know and did not want to know, she just wanted it all to end. She did not want to be anymore. She lifted her head up, looked around the room, a gun she thought, a knife, pills, anything. She sat on the bed. What am I thinking? What am I going to do?

She was paralyzed in this bizarre ugly reality. Caught in a cramp between the polar opposites of love and hate.

Rachel watched her husband adjust his tie in the mirror. She felt disgusted, having sex with him the night before, sex that was no different for him, but to her was a personal violation, an assault, an unequivocal violation of her soul, after the experience she had with the Sheriff. Her previous life, now an abhorrence to her. She had prostituted herself for 16 years and she knew it and she could not stand it. She could not live like this anymore. No, now, she wanted to be worth something, something more than a trophy wife, more than the pleasure she provided in exchange for a sought after life style. She didn't believe in love, thought it just a foolishness of the gullible. So she married for money, for status, wealth and position. But now, she had experienced a brief moment of overwhelming passion and unrequited love for a man, and nothing could ever be the same again. It was as if a river of purity had flowed through her. Love was real, it was all encompassing, overpowering and purifying. It cleansed her life and started all anew.

Love is, the driving primal force of life and by her own doing, she had been starved of it her entire life. Now she wanted love more than she wanted anything in this world, she would not and could not be denied any further.

"Filthy Lucre" the phrase repeated in her mind, over and over, until now she had sold herself for filthy lucre. She could not bear it any longer. Sitting on the edge of the bed, her husband kissed her forehead, "love you Rachel," he said, as he walked out to the kitchen and then on to his car and office. She could not reply. He knew something was amiss, but also assumed it would resolve itself, before he returned ten hours later. But not this time. No, now she would take what she wanted, no more settling, no more enduring him to have cars and trinkets and clothes, no, never again. She thought of her teenage daughter, already off to school, the rebellious daughter who sensed the artificial nature of her parents relationship, even as they, themselves did not. How could she leave, leave her daughter that tied her to a man she did not love, and never did. Her mind raced, she looked at the luggage in the closet, some still unpacked from girls camp, she looked at her clothes, and his. What was she doing?

Was she right to do it? She didn't care, she had to do it! She could not be a kept woman one more day, she could not be his whore a moment longer. She pulled her clothes down off the hangers, breathing heavily, she stuffed them into luggage as she cried, she cried over who she was and what her life had become. This would change, this must change, she would have what she had with the Sheriff, if she must overturn the whole of the earth to get it.

"Base to one, Sheriff? Base to one." Marty tried to radio the Sheriff, locate him to confirm his meeting with the Salt Lake County officers at the airport. There was no response. She starred off out the windows, she thought of her ex husband, how she caught him with her friend, after a night at the bar where she had been a waitress. She thought of the Sheriff, the moment between them, what had come of it? What happened on that mountain, why was he so cold, so aloof, not his normal self. "Base to one, Sheriff, come in. Base to one, Sheriff? Jeff, please answer! Please!" She released the transmitter as a tear fell on her desk. She knew something was wrong, very wrong and her world was about to change.

Patrolman Osbourne slowed his highway patrol cruiser as he came upon the scene of the reported accident. He radioed in, "Yeah, I'm going to need a flat bed wrecker and an ambulance at mile marker 95 I-15 northbound. We've got a roll over and it looks bad." Osborne was over weight, he worried about passing his next physical, about potentially losing his job. He climbed out of his patrol car and began to walk toward the mangled vehicle approximately 100 yards off the right shoulder of the freeway. "Damn" he exclaimed, the barbed wire fence was too tall for him to climb over, he walked back to the right nearly 200 yards where the vehicle had mowed down the fence line, as he did he noticed the drainage culvert where the vehicle struck, "that's going to have to be fixed" he said, a major portion of the dirt had blasted out with the impact of the vehicle. As he walked toward the mangled wreckage he was walking in a debris field, papers, a shot gun, small traffic cones, flares and several three ring binders that had the Iron County seal on them and said Sheriffs Department below the seal. My God he thought, is this a county Sheriff? As he came to the vehicle he could see that indeed it was the color of an Iron County Patrol truck. The cab of the truck was smashed into nothing more than a pile of rubble. He looked inside to see an obviously deceased body, crushed and mangled within the wreckage. It was a male and yes, he was wearing the Iron County Sheriff's uniform. He reached for the name tag, still pinned to the blood soaked torn shirt. It read Sheriff Jeff Lynn.

"The Love of Many Shall Wax Cold"
Chapter 11

She stared straight ahead, oblivious to all around her. The Governor rambled on philosophical in the eulogy of her husband, Sheriff Jeff Lynn, the first Iron County Sheriff killed in the line of duty since the late 1800s. The cause as yet was unclear, he appeared to have lost control of the vehicle at high speed, the highway patrol forensic team estimated speed in excess of 135mph. General Motors had been called in to investigate a potential uncontrolled acceleration problem with the software in their latest fuel injection system. He had made no call in of a high speed pursuit, but equally as troubling, the vehicles computer system registered no record of brakes being applied. The truck had plowed into a dirt embankment at nearly 140 mph and no brakes had been applied. The accident made no sense to anyone but his widow, who sat silent in the nearly three hour long funeral, enduring the attempts of dignitaries from law enforcement, state and county officials to honor her unfaithful husband, the dead Sheriff with the stellar record and career.

She shook hands, accepted hugs from people she had known all her life, but barely recognized on this day. Her mind so stressed and so far off, going over the many years with the only man she had ever loved. A horse draw carriage carried the casket to the cemetery, the funeral procession trailed nearly a mile through the streets of Cedar City. This funeral was the biggest event anyone could remember. State dignitaries and a twenty one gun salute. She stared blankly as they lowered the casket into the ground. People saying their goodbyes, leaving the cemetery and still she stood, staring at the grave. Her bishop and her sister, tried to move her away, but she would not be moved. They retreated to their cars and waited, giving her the time they thought she needed. More than two hours later, she collapsed to her hands and knees, grabbing anything she could and throwing it at the grave. Her sister ran to her side, holding her as she collapsed sobbing in her arms. Nothing in her life had prepared her for this moment and it was more than she could bear. Yet bear it she must, because she was still here and there was no escape from the death of her husband and what he had done with that woman at the girls camp. Betrayal and death, in the same moment in time, she could not endure it.

Her sister and brother in law, picked her up and carried her to their car. At home they placed her on the guest bed. "Should we call the hospital" the sister asked? "No," her husband said, "give her some time, give her tonight, stay with her through the night, I'll spell you in a couple hours." The night was long, no one got much sleep, still she stared at the ceiling, saying nothing. Two days passed, she did not leave the room. Her entire existence was now locked in a state of grief and rage, combined into one paralyzing excruciating cramp, that she came to know as her life.

She looked out at the world through pain stained eyes. Nothing she did, or heard, or saw, or felt, was without this penetrating dark pain. Her only relief was sleep, but reality pounced upon her as she awoke, this thick dark covering of her life, from which there was no escape. Adultery, her husbands adultery, had spawned this evil that destroyed him and left her in this private hell. She lived alone, her husbands pension and death benefits were auto deposited in her accounts. She only went out for groceries and other necessities, avoided family, friends, refused offers of help. She sunk into her anger and grief, as if sinking into a pit of tar with no escape. Never a moment was, that this adultery, this death, did not dominate her mind, her life. She had stopped asking how or why, she didn't care anymore, it simply was, and nothing would change it, and it would not go away.

Rachel checked into the Bellagio on the Las Vegas strip, a corner suite. She stood at the large floor to ceiling windows looking out at the world, bewildered. How did she get here? Her daughter would be home from school now, her husband to follow in a few hours. Should she call them? Could she? What would she say? How could she leave her daughter? She couldn't, but neither could she stay in her former life, trying to pretend she was in love with that lawyer, that, phony semblance of a man. There were no answers. The death of the Sheriff had completely destroyed her previous thoughts for her life, for her life with him. It threw her into turmoil. Her one experience of love, gone, like ash blown away in the hot wind. The, almost forced moment of passion between her and the Sheriff, the absolute release of what felt like years of enslavement, years of degrading private thoughts of herself, freedom from all of that, was now gone in an instant and now only this, this empty world. It had all turned so bad, so fast, such brutal consequences for what seemed so right, so liberating and so awakening and then suddenly so dark, so oppressive. She could make no sense of it.

Her cell phone rang, it was her daughter, she picked it up, "Hi dear." "Mom, where are you?" "I'm just out dear, what do you need." "Emily wants me to come over and spend the night." "On a school night?" "Yes mom, obviously, it's Tuesday." "I'm ok with it dear, just leave a note for your father." "Ok thanks mom, I love you!" "I love you too dear." She looked at the floor, and thought of those words. "I love you." I love you, what did that mean? She sat on the bed, looking at her phone, thinking of her life and her life altering moment on the mountain with the Sheriff. It was as if she were two different people leading two different lives. She could go back, back to her husband, back to her daughter and her life, as far as she knew, no one knew anything. The Sheriff was dead, had he confessed to his wife? Did his wife know? Of course she knew, she saw it in her eyes, when they met, while loading kids into cars to get them off the mountain. It was known between the two women. But was this in some way related to the accident that had killed the Sheriff? Deep down inside, she feared it was, she came to the realization that she knew it was.

"My God! What have I done," she cried. She curled up on the bed, and began sobbing, what have I done?   What have I done? She thought of the bottle of sleeping pills in her over night bag. She thought of her only daughter, the damage she would do to her, the damage she has already done. "And for what," she asked to no one there, "for what" she screamed at the top of her lungs! "16 years of marriage for money! 16 years of marriage for status! 16 years of a loveless marriage to a lawyer I despise and for what, to be here now? My life didn't need to be like this! Why! Why! Why this! God damn it why! This didn't have to be! What is the matter with me! Why, why?"

The consequences of her calculated life, all came crashing down upon her now. For one moment, for the first time in her life, she had passion, pure raw passion and all consuming love for a man. It was an experience that overwhelmed her entire sense of self, but also painfully showed her how pathetic and anemic her calculated materialistic life had been. How her carefully planned life decisions based on wealth, status and life style had robbed her of the fullness of life, the love, the devotion and compassion that starts and sustains a marriage, a family. And now this wonderful man, that had saved her, had given her this brief life changing moment, this short happy life, he was now dead! My God the cruel irony in it! The crushing irony! She sobbed heavily on the bed, not wanting to live, not wanting to be. How did it get like this? Why is he dead? Why did he do that? My God why did he do that? There were no answers, no clarity, only the unbearable weight of what she had done, what they had done and the awful consequences of it.

"Why me" she asked? She knew many women who had affairs, none of them suffered like this, none of their men died! "God why me? Why me? What did I do, what did I do, what did I do." The pillow was wet with tears, she tore at her clothes, she would run though the window, if she could, fall to her death below on the hot asphalt of the Las Vegas strip below. There among the flyers for strippers and whores, where she belonged, there with the rest of the trash, stepped on by stupid tourist intent upon wasting their lives in this hell hole of a town. "Why" she asked, "Why?" The awful consequences, the weight of what she had done, her life, not only the adultery with the Sheriff, but selling herself in a loveless marriage for 16 years, the terror of how she had lived her life, tore at what was left of her heart, her soul. She could not forgive herself, she would not forgive herself.

Marty slid her black dress off, having just returned from the funeral. She was bewildered, lost, what had happened? All of it was so different now. She slipped her jeans on, pulled a sweatshirt over her head, slid her feet into her tennis shoes and left them untied. She walked to the kitchen. How could he be dead? He was just here! The man who had given her a chance, a way to escape the bar life, a way to escape the kind of men he often arrested on a Saturday night. How could he be gone? We were just getting close! She looked around the room, the cheap table and chairs, the linoleum floor and apartment grade countertops. She began to cry. Not for Sheriff Jeff Lynn, but for the loss of Sheriff Jeff Lynn, and all he had meant in her life. He was more than a boss, he was a way out, a way out of the only life she had ever known. She had always felt she was better than the bars, the boyfriends, the broken down cars and cheap housing. She was born too beautiful for this to be her life but somehow, it was her life. The mean streets of these small towns were resentful and ruthless to beautiful young girls. The Sheriff had shown her a way out, had given her a chance, a job with a future and now he was gone, it was all gone. It was no good.

She walked into the bathroom, looked in the mirror, she was not a teen beauty queen anymore. She looked closer to 40 than 30 she thought, the rough life, the drinking, the drugs, the men, it had taken a toll on her and now, the future was altered yet again, and not for the better, by the death of a man who had given her hope. Tears rolled down her cheeks, cheap masquer running down her face. She began to sob heavily, falling back on the bed, "why" she asked, "why me? Why is this my life, why such a mess, why, why can't things just be right for once?" She rolled over and buried her face in her hands, crying heavily. She would lay there until the early evening, then she got up, looked in the mirror at her make up smeared face and thought, my God what a pathetic and hideous thing I've become, preying on another woman's husband, and now he's dead. I am, what they say I am. What the hell is wrong with me? She cried not for Jeff Lynn, but the loss of Jeff Lynn, and the fear of falling back into the life he had rescued her from.

Return to the Cave

Chapter 12

The photograph had made national news. The AP picked it up and it spread like wild fire across the media. A never seen before animal, a large animal, a predator thought to have gone extinct more than ten thousand years ago. How could it now exist in the mountains of central Utah? Where did it come from, how did it get there? Are there more? The questions were many but the reality was undeniable, there it was, a 960 pound lion, closer to the size of a horse than a cougar, with jaws and fangs like a prehistoric saber toothed tiger, unbelievable and yet, it was here, killed on Cedar Mountain at a girls camp. The scientific community was abuzz with excitement. The first new major discovery of this kind in decades.

The body of the cat was frozen in a locker at the Biology Sciences Department of the University of Utah. Debates were already raging about autopsies and the rights to possession and kind and manner of studies. In the silent background, underneath all this excitement, was the reality of retrieving the body of a dead college Professor and finding a couple that went missing at the Brianhead ski resort.

Members of the Salt Lake County SWAT team were flown down to Cedar City to retrieve the body of Professor Dreyfus, last seen in the cave at the top of the lava field near Radar Peak. The group met at the Iron County Sheriffs office with Marty acting as communications coordinator and facilitator for local services. Donald Brown, the cougar tracker, was called in as the only remaining survivor and witness to what had transpired on that mountain, in that cave, when Professor Dreyfus died. Officer Bill Clancy, the head of the SWAT Team, had requested Donalds presence when his team entered the cave. Donald flatly refused, he had hunted cougar nearly all his life, but this was no cougar and nothing had ever terrified him more than those moments he had spent in that cave with Sheriff Lynn and Professor Dreyfus. Being pursued inside the confines of that cave, was not something he ever wanted to do again. The nightmares of it had kept him up at night. The meeting convened in the conference room at the Iron County Sheriffs office.

"Mr. Brown," officer Clancy said, "may I call you Donald?" "Please!" Donald replied. "Donald, I'm told by the biologist that it's highly likely the lion that Sheriff Lynn killed on Cedar Mountain was the only one, a genetic anomaly, a defect of birth if you will, a freak of nature caused by some genetic mutation in a local cougar, that it's highly unlikely there are others, therefore that cave should be empty of anything other than Professor Dreyfus remains. We would like you to accompany us, show us the way, the State will pay whatever fee you charge." Donald looked up at officer Clancy and said, "sir, that may well be, but I don't think your going to find any remains. Have you seen the cat the Sheriff killed?" "Yes I have," Clancy replied, "it is indeed impressive, I've never seen anything like it." "Neither have I Officer Clancy and I never want to see one again," said Donald. "The only reason we got out of that cave alive was because that cat was busy ripping the Professor to pieces! And let me tell you, until you are there, experience that, you can't remotely understand. Don't give me any of your bravery Bull Shit, because you don't know! You don't know!" "I understand Donald, but that cave has not been mapped and we need some local expertise familiar with the area." Donald looked at the floor, shook his head and said no, you don't understand. He looked up and said, "Look, I'll ride up in the helicopter with you, I'll tell you everything I know, but I'm not saying I'll go in that cave. I'm no coward, I've hunted big cats all my life, but my gut tells me if you go in there, there is a good chance you won't be coming out. My gut is generally right." Officer Clancy looked at him with a stern eye and said, "nothing on this planet could survive the fire power we are bringing into that cave Donald, but I guess we go with what we've got. You can guide us on the radio if you feel so compelled. Meet us at the airport 9am tomorrow morning, bring your GPS dog tracker. Marty, will you get us three rooms at the best local motel?" "Certainly" she replied.

Donald looked up and said, "one more thing Clancy, the lion in the cave, had my dogs GPS tracker inside it, the one the Sheriff killed, did not. Your biologist are full of shit, there is more than one." Officer Clancy looked at his SWAT officers, both with a look of concern on their face, and said, "regardless Donald, we're going to retrieve that body and we will kill anything that tries to stop us."

The following morning the Salt Lake County SWAT Team loaded their gear into the helicopter at the Cedar City Airport. Donald arrived with his GPS monitor and greeted Officer Clancy who handed him a small monitor screen. He yelled over the sound of the helicopter warming up, "this is a monitor to our body cams. You will be able to watch our progress into the cave and speak to us directly through our radios. You won't need to go into the cave." "Thank you," said Donald, "but I still think it's a bad idea going back in there!" Officer Clancy smiled and nodded his head, "that's why we get paid the big bucks!" Donald shook his head looking at the ground. Officer Clancy slapped him on the shoulder and yelled, "come on, let's go get what's left of Dreyfus!"

The men boarded the helicopter, two SWAT team members Officer Clancy and Donald. Putting on their head sets the pilot looked back and said, "nice to see you again Mr. Brown! I hope we have a better day than our last trip up!" The helicopter slowly climbed vertical then aggressively banked forward as it began the six thousand foot climb to Radar Peak and the near by lava fall. It was a calm Cedar City morning as Donald looked out the window as they passed over the city and started the climb up over the mountain. A large herd of deer were feeding in a meadow just above the city. Low for this time of year Donald thought, usually they're in the upper Right Hand Canyon area near the stream. "Have you got any signal on the GPS yet," Officer Clancy asked Donald? "No was his reply, but we won't until we get near the mouth of the cave, and even then, the batteries on the collars are probably dead by now. Really Clancy! Donald yelled back, I don't have a good feeling about this! Let's just say we found nothing and call it a day!" "You know I can't do that" replied Officer Clancy.

The helicopter banked over Radar Peak and flew to the east over Brianhead ski resort and to the lava ridge where Professor Dreyfus was last seen alive. The pilot yelled over the intercom, "given the circumstances, I'm going to hover over that rock again like last time, you guys bail out, I'll move back and hold just off the ridge." "Ok" Officer Clancy yelled back, "activate body cams! Donald?" Clancy yelled. "Can you see the cams on that monitor?"

"Yes," Donald replied, "all three split screen." "You can get full screen by touching any one of them, push the black button on the side to talk," yelled Clancy. "Got it!" Donald replied. "Have you got anything on your GPS?" Asked Clancy! Donald checked. "Yes, Missy and Max, they're dead inside the cave, Max is right before where we lost Dreyfus. If there's anything left of him it should be just beyond that, you'll see the head of a hound with the collar still on the neck on the right side of the floor of the cave, not much further, maybe 20 yards is where the cat got Dreyfus. And I've got Toby as well Officer Clancy, that lion is in there, but further back, way further back, a mile or more! That cave must go on much further! You're only going in about a hundred yards. But for sure, this is not the one Jeff Lynn killed at the girls camp! There is another lion in there, it's not moving but it's in there! You better not go in there!" Said Donald. "You're jumping to conclusions" yelled Officer Clancy! Donald yelled back, "don't bet your life on it!"

With that the pilot put the right skid on the lava rock and the men climbed out of the helicopter. Clancy and his two men worked their way toward the mouth of the lava tube cave while the pilot backed the helicopter off the rock and out about 100 yards off the ridge holding in a level hover. Clancy radioed to Donald. "Can you read me over the monitor?" Donald could not hear him over the noise of the helicopter. Clancy pointed to his ears which Donald saw on the monitor. He plugged his head phones into the monitor, pushed the button on the side and asked if the SWAT team could hear him. They each answered yes. Clancy told Donald, "watch your GPS, if Toby starts to move you notify us immediately!" "Understood!" Donald replied. Each of the three men looked down at the mangled remains of the hound dogs as they worked their way into the cave. Donald watched intently on the monitor. After a few minutes Donald radioed Clancy, "that is my dog Max on the right, Professor Dreyfus was last seen about 20-30 yards further into the cave." "Copy," replied Clancy. The three men worked their way further into the cave, their head lamps brightly illuminating the oblong shape of the cave. "Nothing yet Donald, we're going further in." "Copy!" Donald replied. "Any movement on Toby?" asked Clancy. "No!" Donald replied. "That lion is showing up quite a distance from where you are now, if I had to guess I'd say a mile or more! It might be dead, I emptied my .50 cal at it when it attacked the Professor." "Good" Clancy replied! "We will keep going!" Donald said, "I have no idea how much further that cave goes, but it might be tied into Mammoth Cave, which is a good five miles off to the east." "Copy that Donald! We're not here to explore caves, once we get the body of Dreyfus we will leave the cave mapping to the spelunkers."

Further into the cave the three men went with their M4 rifles, short barrel shot guns and .45 pistols all off safety, fully loaded and ready for extreme conflict if need be. They were supremely confident in their ability to kill anything that comes their way. Two hundred yards in and Clancy reported nothing still. Donald replied, "I told you Officer Clancy, that cat ate Dreyfus, there is nothing left!" Just then the officer on camera two cried out! "Wait! There is something, to the left!" Donald switched to camera two on his monitor. As the officer approached, he stated, "it's a human head!" It was tangled and matted hair, it was blonde hair, there was a head, neck, partial shoulder and arm of a young woman with blonde hair on the floor of the cave against the left wall. The eye's staring blankly into the light. "That's not Dreyfus!" Stated Clancy. The three men stood and stared at the remains, after a tense moment, Clancy said, "bag it!" He radioed to Donald, "have your Sheriff's Secretary call my office, I want the forensics team waiting, I want the University of Utah DNA people on this immediately. We've got multiple victims and an active predatory animal on this mountain, we've got to close this area off immediately!" "Will do," Donald replied. Just as he glanced to the GPS monitor he saw the GPS for Toby start to move! The lion was not dead, it was on the move.

"Clancy!" Donald yelled into the radio! "Get the hell out of there! The cat is on the move!" Clancy yelled "holy shit! Get her in the bag! We gotta get out of here!" The remains were shoved in the body bag, it was thrown over the shoulder of one of the officers as the three men started to run out of the cave. Double timing it Clancy yelled "give me the bag, cover our backs!" Clancy, drawing on his college football days took off in a full sprint that the other men could not stay with, adrenaline pumping and driving every stride, he sprinted like never before, with the remains of what was once a beautiful girl, held under his arm like a football. Donald radioed Clancy, "it's not moving toward you! It's moving away!" Clancy and his men were in full speed all out sprint, they heard nothing but their own lungs gasping for air. The men kept running. The pilot moved the helicopter to the lava rock. Clancy had put fifty yards between himself and the other men by the time he reached the mouth of the cave with the woman's remains under his arm. He turned and drew his M4 rifle down upon the blackness behind him, his men both appeared out of the darkness, gasping heavily in the thin high altitude air. Get in the chopper! Clancy yelled, take the remains! Once the two men were on board, he lowered the barrel of the rifle and climbed his way back into the helicopter. The pilot pulled off the rock and Donald yelled "wait!" The pilot held position. Donald yelled "the cat is moving south east, slowly. Wait, give me time to zoom this out! I don't want to lose the signal! It looks like he's moving toward Mammoth cave, these caves must be connected. Mammoth cave is near Duck Creek! We've got to warn those people, there are hundreds of cabins at Duck Creek!" "We will Donald, we will!" Yelled Clancy, gasping for breath! "Pilot!" Yelled Clancy! "Make this thing haul ass! We've got to close this mountain!"

The pilot lowered the nose and pushed the helicopter to near 180 mph. As they approached the airport Clancy yelled "No! Drop us at the Sheriffs office!" The pilot veered off to the left and put the helicopter down in a dirt lot across from the Sheriffs office. Clancy ordered the pilot to keep it running, told his men to stay inside while he and Donald ran across the road to find Marty at her desk doing her nails. "Who took over for Lynn as head of this office," Clancy asked. Marty looked up, "well, no one has officially been assigned to replace Jeff but Joe Woodard has been filling in for him." "Can you get him in here immediately" asked Clancy, "he's on patrol but I'll try she said," in an irritated voice. Woodard was a few blocks away and pulled into the parking lot less than five minutes later. Joe walked into the office, Clancy said, "I'm Charles Clancy lead officer on the Salt Lake County SWAT Team, I assume you're the active Sheriff in the absence of Sheriff Lynn correct?" "Well, no one has appointed me but I am the most senior officer of the four of us remaining officers." "Ok," said Clancy, "well, we need to shut down the mountain, in particular Duck Creek and Brianhead immediately!" "We already tried that sir," replied Joe. "A judge signed a restraining order preventing us from closing down the mountain." "My god what kind of idiot would do that" yelled Clancy! "The new owners of Brianhead sir, they opposed the shut down saying their business could not lose the summer income." "Can their business survive their guest getting decapitated by a lion?" Yelled Clancy! Officer Woodard looked down, shaking his head, then said, "I was called up there, to find a missing couple, the owners were called and they filled an immediate restraining order against us, Jeff wanted to get everyone off the mountain but the judge shut us down. I never did find that couple," said Woodard. "Well" said Clancy, staring up at the ceiling, "I may have found what's left of your couple, we have a woman's head out in the helicopter!" Woodard looked up and asked "blonde?" "Yes!" Clancy replied. "I think the parents are still at Brianhead," said Woodard. "Well, no one is seeing those remains until we identify who that is," said Clancy.

"Look!" Said Clancy, "I don't have authority to order you to close the mountain, but I'm telling you there is another lion on the loose and the GPS was tracking it toward Duck Creek. I've got a dead body and a helicopter waiting on me. You guys figure it out. I'm going back to Salt Lake and I'll try and get you some additional help down here. This problem is not over!"

With that Clancy slammed the door and ran back to the waiting helicopter. Donald looked at Marty and

Officer Woodard, "I'm just a tracker he said! Here! Take my GPS. I'm done with this shit, I'm done with hunting, I'm out of it! That lion is up near Duck Creek, I don't know what else to tell you. Do whatever you have to, but if you don't do something, more people will die." Marty and Woodard looked at each other, both feeling lost without Sheriff Lynn.

A New Challenge
Chapter 13

The helicopter eased on to the roof of the Salt Lake County General hospital. The helipad crew ran out to meet the arriving flight crew, but Officer Clancy ignored them. He climbed out, reached into the back, pulled out the black body bag containing the partial remains of the woman they had found in the cave and put it under his arm. He yelled to one of the attendants, "what floor is the morgue on?" "Basement level three" was the response. He walked deliberately past the gurney and waiting staff, went straight to the elevators, pushed B-3 and looked in the mirror, as the doors closed. What he saw disturbed him. He was head of SWAT because of his calm focused demeanor, his cool under pressure, his numerous acts of courage under fire, his ability to think clearly in chaos. But never in his life had he ever imagined running out of a cave, absolutely terrified, carrying a dead body, while being chased, by some monstrous beast. The experience shook him, left a mark on his soul, an expression remained on his face, here in this elevator, some three hours later. His confidence was shattered, his faith in himself damaged, he was a war veteran, a combat solider, but never had he ran, he had never experienced primal fear like this. It was as if some primitive instinct had awoke in him, chemically altered his brain and in fact, it had. He thought of the tracker, Donald Brown's arguments to not go back in that cave, he now understood, he wished he had listened. He now knew he had to live the rest of his life, having experienced something he did not understand or knew existed prior to this day but had altered who he thought, he was. He was over confident, now he knew real fear, real terror. He was a changed man, and it concerned him, how it would affect the rest of his life, his job, his relationship with his wife, his children. His one free hand was shaking, as he stared at himself in the mirror.

The bell rang, the elevator reached Basement floor 3, the morgue. Clancy carried the body bag to the front desk like it was a sack of cement. He looked at the admittance clerk still seated at her desk and said, "this is evidence, these remains are critically important evidence, I need them secured in a locked storage locker, I need the receipt and full custody transfer documentation." The over weight elderly black woman looked up at him and said, "sir, they are all important to us. Please take a seat and I'll be with you in a minute." "No!" Clancy yelled! The adrenaline of the previous hours still driving him. The woman was startled! Clancy saw it and immediately felt bad for frightening the woman. "Look" he said, in a calmer voice, "I'm sorry, but this is an emergency, a lot of people are at risk, please secure these remains, give me the documentation, I need to report back to the chief of police!" She looked up at him and calmly asked, "and who are you?" "I'm Captain Bill Clancy of the Salt Lake County Special Weapons and Tactics group. I have the remains of a woman that has been killed by a large lion which is still on the loose in the mountains near Cedar City. We must get a response team on the mountain immediately. Please process these remains." She looked at him in the same blank manner, intent upon proving to him that his yelling and flaunt of apparent authority, had no affect on her, and so she said again, "Have a seat Bill."

Clancy stood at the counter and cursed under his breath. Then realizing his radio was now back in range of his office he called in, "41 to Base." "Base, 41," was the reply. "Carolyn will you call Tess Anderson's office, she's the head of public safety, tell her we have a public emergency in Iron County that needs an immediate response. See if you can arrange a meeting with her and ask her to include George Smith, chief over at State Patrol." "Will do Bill, Base out, 41 out." He turned his attention back to the Admittance Clerk. She rose from the desk and walked to Clancy, peering over the counter she asked, "where is the body?" "In the bag," he said as he lifted the crumpled bag off the floor. "Is it an infant" she asked? "No, it's a head, a shoulder and an arm." She looked at him with a scowl. "Well," she said, "you're going to need a nurse to place the remains on an autopsy table and fill out the intake forms and properly label the body before we can store the remains here." "Ok lady, I don't think you understand," he said in a raised voice. She responded immediately in an equally stern voice, "no, I perfectly understand the procedures of this hospital. If you don't like them, then you can find yourself another hospital!" Rage began to rise in Clancy, he looked at the woman, bitting his lip he then looked at the floor. He radioed the chopper, "41 to 46," "46 copy," "yeah Jeremy, take the chopper back to base, call it a day, looks like I'm going to be here a while." "Affirmative Bill, let us know if you need anything," was the reply. "41 out," "46 clear." Clancy looked up at the woman and smiled, OK, "let's get this done, your way!"

The phone rang a fifth time as Marty reached for it, she had been in the break room getting another cup of coffee, she was hoping it was not a state official, so many had been calling lately, she knew the phones were to be answered promptly, no more than three rings, but she was the only one in the office, no one had yet been assigned to replace Sheriff Lynn. It was Doug Williams on the phone, a resident of Duck Creek. He asked to speak to the Sheriff. "I'm sorry sir, no one is in the office right now, can I take a message and have an officer get back to you?" "Well," said Doug, "I've got something on one of my security cameras you guys are going to want to see! I can't tell what it is but it's big, and it's not a moose, deer, elk or bear! The thing has a tail on it like a cougar, but it's back is as high as the hood of my truck!" "Have you seen the news lately Mr.

Williams?" Asked Marty. "No!" Was his firm reply, "I stay up here to avoid the news." "Ok, well, do you have a way to email me this photo?" "Yes, I can send it now," he replied, "but I also want to report my dog missing. He's a Rottweiler, his chain must have broke in the night. We leave him out to keep the deer and raccoons out of our garden but he's gone." "Ok Mr. Willams," said Marty, "I'll make a note of it." "Do you want an officer to come to your home, fill out a report?" "No," he said, "I just want you guys to be aware of what showed up on my security camera, if that's a cougar, it's the biggest damned cougar I've ever seen! And if it took my dog, you guys need to kill it and I mean like right now! We can't have a beast like that roaming around up here!" "Yes sir, you're absolutely right Mr. Williams, one hundred percent! I'll have an officer review your photo and we will get somebody on it right away!" Said Marty. "Ok, well, give me that email address and I'll forward it now. My wife is scared out of her mind, she wants to go back to Las Vegas!" Williams replied. "I understand," said Marty, "it might not be a bad idea to get off the mountain until we can resolve this matter." "I'm not getting off the mountain," replied Williams, "no damn animal is driving me out of my home. You sons of bitches just get up here and kill this thing or I will! Got it?"

With that the old man slammed down the phone. Marty stared off into space, without Sheriff Lynn, everything was just a mess, a mess and she didn't know what to do about it. She looked at the office email and there was the picture, it was dark and grainy but yes, there it was, exactly as the old man had said. She stared at it for a moment and it scared her, something is out there, something real and somebody has to kill it, but who?

The public safety meeting was held in the conference room at the governors office. State public safety officials, police, state patrol, national guard, department of wild life, local politicians and several business leaders. The Governor had called the meeting because this story of a prehistoric lion had made national and international news. It was giving the state of Utah, a state that billed itself as a world wide destination for outdoor recreation and travel, a bad reputation. This so called lion was killing tourist and the tourist industry.

The Governor opened the meeting by saying, "we've got a problem, a big problem down in Cedar City, somebody released their freak circus lions in our mountains and they're killing people. There are now five deaths attributed to this lion or these lions, there are now confirmed at least two lions in the central mountains area. The one Sheriff Lynn killed and one that showed up on a security camera in Duck Creek, a small cabin community located between Zions Canyon and Bryce's Canyon, two of the most visited National Parks in the country." The Governor told the group of state and business officials, "people don't go camping with the lions in Africa, they're going to find someplace else for their summer vacations if Utah is not a safe place to be! We've got to kill or capture these damn things and make a very public announcement that our state is safe!" "Kill or capture?" The Salt Lake County Sheriff said. "Did you get a look at that thing at the U? They had to make a special freezer for it! Hell they've got biologist from all over the world coming to examine it. We are famous alright, famous for that horse sized cougar the University is so damn proud of!"

"Look" said the Governor, "I'm under enormous pressure not to kill whatever it is out there, the scientific community is just beside themselves with this new discovery. In the mean time we're finding mangled body parts of tourist scattered in cave systems that we advertise on our tourism web site! For people to come explore! For gawds sake! We have to assure the public that these things are not loose roaming the night waiting to drag them out of their tents and RVs! How are we going to do that?"

"I'm not sure we can Governor," said the head of Parks and Recreation for Iron County. "Yellowstone has Grizzly and wolves, they still get plenty of tourist, maybe we're thinking of this in the wrong way, maybe we need to bill it as a tourist attraction instead."

"Yellowstone does not have five dead tourist and other people missing in the span of three weeks Jerry! Think again! I want this damn beast dead and I want it dead now! Our tourism numbers are taking a real hit. I'm in the middle of a legal battle with the damn ski industry who has a restraining order preventing us from shutting down Brianhead, if you can believe that foolishness! We can't let this thing continue to kill people while the courts and our agencies take their sweet ass time thinking about it!"

"Here's a thought," said Rachel Bailey the head of tourism. "We apparently have a living dinosaur in our state, we are famous for dinosaur attractions, let's capture this cat, or these cats, and put them in the Hogle Zoo." "Again! Have you seen that thing Rachel?" Interrupted the Salt Lake Sheriff. "No" she said, "but I agree, if this really is an ancient animal, we should not kill it." Ray Ferguson, head of the department of Wild Life, asked the Governor, "what makes you think these are circus lions?" The Governor shook his head, "I don't know what they are. The University has come up with this fantastic story that they are South American Saber Tooth Tigers, thought to have been extinct for more than ten thousand years. That's just foolishness to me, there is something more to this, there is no way those are ancient tigers somehow brought back to life, here, in our state, that's just craziness. Maybe some idiot cloned them and turned them loose! Who the hell knows! What I think is the University's biology department is looking for more attention, more federal grant money. But whatever those cats are, wherever they came from, they're out of control and we are losing money hand over fist because of all this sensationalism. For tourist, we've become the place to avoid, we can't have that!"

The Governor looked back at Rachel, "they catch grizzly bears in Yellowstone, with big barrel traps, I've seen it on TV. Lets get ahold of those people!" Turning to his staff, "find out who catches grizzlies in Yellowstone. Get those people on the phone." "Sir, said the Sheriff, this ain't no grizzly bear! It won't fit in those traps!" "Then we will build bigger traps!" Yelled the Governor. The Sheriff, looked down and shook his head, "and until then?" "Well, apparently they've been here a while, it's only been the last few weeks that we've had a problem. "No, this is the answer," the Governor said, "even if we kill them, we can't be sure there are not more, the answer is to capitalize on this, people get eaten by bears too, we've got an opportunity here, we have a lot of publicity, bad publicity that we need to turn around, we need to make it count!" He turned to his staff again, "get the Yellowstone people on the phone immediately. That is the answer, trap them, put them in the zoo, people will come from all over, stay in the hotels, eat in the restaurants. People will pay to see a real living prehistoric cat, a Saber Tooth Tiger! Once they've become normalized to these animals, these circus lions, clones, mutant prehistoric beast, whatever they are, they will be no different than the bears in Yellowstone. Our outdoor industry will return, it will just take a little time. We will be like Yellowstone, no different."

"Anybody have anything else?" Asked the Governor before bringing the meeting to a close, "yes" replied the Salt Lake County Sheriff. "We've got a 30 year old bar maid trying to run the Sheriffs office down in Cedar, no one has been assigned to replace Sheriff Lynn, can you appoint an interim Sheriff until their county commission can get their act together and appoint a new Sheriff?" "Yes" said the Governor, "pick your best man and send him down, my staff will supply him with the paper work."

With that, he walked away from the podium and looked down at his 22 year old blonde intern sitting behind the podium, he leaned over and said, "get us a room at the Grand, I need a break from all this." She smiled, knowing that room would be money in the bank for her, in the not too distant future. She pushed stop on her phone, that had been recording the entire meeting. As she started to walk out, she glanced back over her shoulder and noticed three men in the room admiring her form as she walked out of the room. "So easy, she said, so easy."

Trapping A Ghost

Chapter 14

"What the hell is that? Jeez, you've got yourself a big kitty here, where in all creation did you find this son bitch?" Asked Bob Johnson the Montana trapper hired by the state of Utah to capture the lions loose in the central mountains of Iron County. "Smilodon S. Populator," proudly said Dr. Wayne Hemplestead, director of the Zoology Department at the University of Utah. "It's a darn shame they killed it, this literally was a living fossil, a living version of what's commonly known as the Saber Tooth Tiger, the South American version." Bob looked at the Professor, "how do you know that," he asked? "Well, we've done extensive genetic testing, it's not a perfect match, in fact it's not a match to anything, but the codes align most closely with the Smilodon, the South American genus." "How did it get here," asked Bob? "We have no idea," the Professor admitted. "There is much speculation about that answer, some say it was cloned, some say they never went extinct, we are doing further genetic testing to try and answer that question, but for now, here it is, killed by a Sheriff who was an incredibly good shot with a 9mm pistol." "What the hell!" Exclaimed Bob. "Somebody shot this with a 9mm?" "Yes, four shots, right into the orbitals, where the skull was the thinnest. Had he missed the eyes, the bullets would have likely glanced off the thick hard bone of the skull, a skull evolved for fighting with other huge cats. Instead the bullets went directly into the brain cavity, longitudinally, massive destruction to the grey matter of the brain. A real shame, we could have learned so much from a biopsy of that brain!" "Where is this guy, I'd like to meet him," said Bob. "Unfortunately he died in a car accident, very troubling, the only person to have a direct confrontation with the species and survive. Well, actually there is another, a cougar tracker in Cedar City, but he is not talking, no doubt traumatized by the event."

"Jeez I can't get over how big that cat is," said Bob. "Yes, just over five feet at the shoulder, 960 pounds, and it's a female." "You've got to be kidding" said Bob, "you mean there is a male out there, likely larger than this?" "We don't know," said the Professor, "we do have a partial photograph of one, taken at night by a security camera, but only the back half of the torso, it is taller than the truck hood it was walking past, so yes, likely bigger than this one." "Well," said Bob, "I have a grizzly bear trap on the back of my flat bed, but it's not big enough. "No", said Bob, "these are bigger than polar bears, and look at the shoulder muscle on that thing, that's bigger than any polar bear I've ever seen." "Yes," said the Professor, "clearly with claws and fangs like that, this cat was built for grasping large animals, very large animals, like the prehistoric Buffalo, which were significantly larger than our current species of Buffalo." "And the fangs!" Said Bob, "those are like swords!" "Yes" the Professor agreed, "hence the name, Saber Tooth!"

"Well," said Bob, "I've got to build a bigger trap, this is a bigger animal than I was led to believe, the Governor is going to have to come up with more money." "I don't think that is going to be a problem," replied the Professor. "The bigger issue is time, these cats pose a serious risk to the public, the Governor wants them taken out of the mountains, alive." "Well" said Bob, "what the Governor wants and what the Governor gets, may be two different things. I've trapped polar bear, some over a thousand pounds, but none have shoulders, claws and teeth like this thing." "Yes" said the Professor, "it's quite the magnificent specimen, scientists are coming from all over the world to examine it."

"And again," asked Bob, "you have no idea how it got here?" "Well" said the Professor, "off the record, strictly between you and me, not to be repeated? Agreed?" "Yes," said Bob. "Well, we've had an extraordinary amount of genetic mutations of species in the central mountains of Utah, frogs, fish, birds, deer, generating all sorts of abnormalities, we attribute that to the nuclear testing that was done during the 1950s and 60s just to the southwest in Nevada. Central Utah received nuclear fallout as if it had been in ten years of nuclear war. The federal government doesn't want us publicizing our opinions, but as scientist we don't see these genetic anomalies, so often and so rapidly, through so many species, anywhere else in the world like we do here in the central mountain ranges of Utah. My guess, and it's strictly a guess, and will remain so until genetic testing can confirm it, but my guess is this is a genetic anomaly in the local cougar population caused by nuclear fallout. A mother cat, or cats have likely had their genetic code damaged, or altered, and the ancient code, so to speak, for these cats, these Smilodons, from which the North American cougar likely evolved, that ancient genome may have been reactivated in the cougar population of central Utah. Nuclear radiation does strange things to DNA. We've seen huge frogs that don't belong in any frog species that we can compare them to. World record sized fish coming out of relatively small lakes where they should not be. World record sized cougars, coming out of areas that have no particular reason for having such large cats! It's almost as if they have evolved back to their prehistoric ancestors! And now this, a full sized prehistoric Saber Tooth Tiger, killed 20 miles from Cedar City Utah. It's just incredible. The federal government's dirty little nuclear fallout secret is about to be exposed, or so I fear."

"Yes," said Bob, with a look of amazement on his face. "And again," said the Professor, "absolutely not a word." "Oh, certainly not" said Bob, "not like anybody talks to me anyway!" "Well," said the Professor, "if you catch one of these, you'll be on every nightly news in the country, so please, choose your words wisely, what I've told you here, is solely my speculation, nothing further, though I think in time, we will have the evidence to back it up." "Well, that's a big if Professor, like I said, I've been on many hunts and came up empty, until I saw this animal here today, quite frankly, I thought it was all a bunch of BS, a bunch of pansy asses afraid of an over sized cougar, but no, this is the real thing. I'm going to build an oversized polar bear trap, we will give that a go, but even then, with this being a one off deal, I wouldn't bet the farm on catching one." "Well," said the Professor, "when dealing with radiation altered chromosomes, rarely do you find the ability to reproduce, carried into subsequent generations. So even if we don't capture a live specimen, they're likely to die out in the coming generations. It's just impossible to say at the moment."

"Ok, well, I need to get busy on that beast trap. Thank you for letting me see it, I really had no idea, this is like nothing I've ever seen before and I've been trapping griz and polar bear for 40 years. This is just crazy, not something I ever imagined seeing in my life time." "Nor I, said the Professor, strange frogs and oversized fish yes, but this is a historical moment in zoology, in biology, in science! We are incredibly fortunate to have this opportunity." Bob looked at the Professor and said, "I'd bet that colleague of yours didn't feel so fortunate in that cave!" Bob gave the Professor a wink as he walked out. The Professor turned and looked at the floor and said, "no, I don't imagine Ron did."

Bob called his friend in Nome Alaska, a local Native, an Aleuts man named Henry after a British explorer who got in a jam one winter and was helped out by the local tribe. He was so thankful he repaid the tribe by building a generator power plant bringing electricity to the small remote community. Several sons were named Henry in his honor.

"Hey Henry," yelled Bob into the phone, "yeah Bob, you don't have to yell," said Henry, "we've got a new cell tower now." "Oh! Sorry," said Bob. "Hey, well, you remember that big son of a bitch we trapped and killed five, six years ago, the one that killed that old lady out by the dump?" "Yeah, more like ten years ago, but what of it Bob?" "Well, do you still have that trap we built?" "Ah, yeah, last time I looked it was still out by the dump, haven't used it in years." "Will you head out there and see if it's still there and in working order. I've got this damn cat I've got to trap here in Utah," said Bob. "Oh yeah! Read about that," said Henry, "big mean looking son of a bitch." "Yeah, well you ought to see it in person," said Bob, "damn thing is bigger than that bear we got there a few years ago. Got teeth on it like some kind of horror show or something!" "Well sure Bob, I'll check it out but I think the shipping cost might be more than if you built one there! Don't ya think?" Asked Henry. "Well yes but I've got this Governor that's got his panties all in a wad, he wants this cat caught and caught yesterday, he'll probably cover the shipping." "Ok, sure then Bob, but you know, we're going to want it back, then what?" Asked Henry. "You're probably right Henry, I should find me a welding shop here, throw a few hundred extra bucks at them and get it built on the quick." "Yeah Bob! I think that's your best bet. Hell that trap probably weighs ten thousand pounds, remember we built that son of a bitch out of that mining equipment left behind by that idiot that thought he was going to get rich?" "Yeah, your right Henry, I'll get one built here. Ok then."

"How's the Misses?" Asked Bob. "Oh shit Bob, you know, never cuts me a moments slack." "Yeah, I know, laughed Bob. That's why I got rid of mine. God almighty how's a man supposed to live with a woman on his ass 24/7." "Oh yeah, ain't that the truth Bob, but up here, I've got no place to go!" "I hear ya Henry, I hear ya," said Bob. "Listen, if you ever want a job, I can probably keep you busy down here. These limp wrist politicians won't let us kill bear, so we're trapping and hauling the same damn ole sows over and over again. I bet I trap ten bear a season. Pays the bills, I can't complain." "Ok then Bob," said Henry, "I've got this damn snow machine that won't start, son bitchin damned electronic ignition and all you know." "Yeah" said Bob, "points and condensers, going away from that was a big mistake. Well, take care, and keep yer dick out of the mud lest yer ole lady cut it off!" "Oh fer sure fer sure Bob, you know I'm too old for that shit anyway!" Laughed Henry. "True that Henry, true that!" "Ya, see ya now Bob."

With that Bob hung up and looked around the room, he was not familiar with Salt Lake, where to find a welding shop, one that could build his steel cage trap. He thought he might be better off to get it done in Cedar City, they wouldn't be as busy down there. He pulled out the list of contact persons the Governor's office gave him, Marty, Cedar City Sheriffs office, hmmm, she should know!

Trail of Bones
Chapter 15

"Look damn it, I don't think you understand!" Yelled the man on the phone with Marty. "That's two cows! Two cows! Each weighed damn near two thousand pounds! Now you tell me who is stealing my cows in the middle of the night, dragging them over a concrete and steel rail fence? They bent four inch steel rail! Who drags a cow over a fence and how? With a back hoe? In the middle of the night? Who the hell does that?" "Yes sir, I understand" said Marty. "No! I don't think you do! Get somebody up here, get my cows back, or me and my boys will! Do you understand that? Do your damn job! There is some shit going on up here and I'm not going to tolerate it any more! What the hell is the point of having cops if they don't do their damn job?" Yelled the old man.

"Yes sir!" Said Marty. "You're exactly right!" Before she could finish her last sentence the old man slammed down the phone.

Marty winced at the noise in her ear as she put down the phone. She became aware of someone standing at her desk as she finished her note from the phone call. She looked up and was startled to see a young man, a muscular young man in state patrol uniform standing at her desk. "Hi, I'm Chase, I've been assigned as the interim Sheriff for Iron County." Marty was taken aback for a moment, she said nothing. "Here are my assignment papers, signed by the Governor," he said. "Um, well, yes," said Marty, "they seem to be in order as she glanced at the papers." Her mind raced. This was not what she needed right now, an attractive young man around while she was still reeling from the loss of Sheriff Lynn. She realized the awkward moment was building, so she said, "ah, you'll need a desk!" "Yes, I will," he replied. "Well, let me go through Sheriff Lynn's desk, his widow has not been in to collect his things, let me gather his stuff and we will put you in there." "Of course," said Chase, "take your time." He watched her walk across the room, he liked what he saw, wow he thought, Sheriff Clark was right.

Marty could feel his eyes upon her, difficult she thought, this is going to be difficult. She was frustrated, almost angry and confused at the same time, she had to think about this.

She pulled a partially filled dusty box down from the closet and began going through the desk, pictures of Christine Lynn, a pair of gloves, a tooth brush, various odds and ends, a log book with several recent hand written entries, she placed these things in the box. He walked into the room and said, "let me help you with that box." "No!"she said, in an almost angry voice, "no," now speaking in a softer tone, "these things need to go to Sheriff Lynns widow, she hasn't been in yet. I'll see to it that she gets them. Things have been hard, around here, since he's been gone," she said. "Yes" he said, "I can imagine, terrible, that wreck, I read about it, the report." "Yes, it was," Marty said, "Jeff was a good man, a very good man, well liked in the community. We all miss him." "No doubt," said Chase, "no doubt." Their eyes met and she quickly turned away, Chase could sense things were still raw and he didn't know how to react or what to say. Marty returned to her desk and nervously shuffled through the papers as if she were looking for something. Chase sat in

Sheriff Lynns chair and immediately noticed it was worn into another body, the reality of the absent man began to dawn upon him. He looked down at the desk and thought, this is going to be hard.

An idea crossed Marty's mind, the old man yelling at her, earlier on the phone, she would send Chase up there to investigate, get him out of the office, give her time to adjust. "Um, excuse me," Marty said from her desk. "Yes," responded Chase immediately. "What should I call you," Marty asked, "Sheriff Smith?" "Oh, no, said Chase, I'm not a real Sheriff, I've only been assigned temporarily until the Iron County Commission finds a permanent replacement." "Oh, ok," said Marty. "Well, we've got a bit of a problem, we're short manned and we're just getting flooded by calls. I've got a man, up near Duck Creek, he runs a small dairy farm, been up there for years. His name is Ezra Jorgenson. He's missing two cows, he swears they've been stolen and he's threatening to take guns and go looking for them. Can you go up there, talk to him, investigate and take a report, see if you can help him. He was very irate on the phone this morning." "Certainly" Chase said. "Here is the address, if you go right out of the parking lot and head east that will put you on main, then just turn left on 14 and he's just past Duck Creek, about a half hour up the canyon." "Well, thank you, but my truck has GPS." "Oh of course," blushed Marty, "I guess I've been rambling on." "No, not at all" said Chase. "Shall I go up there now?" "Yes if you would please," said Marty. "And please, take your time, he's a very demanding man on the phone, those cows can't be far, if you would see if you can get them back for him." "Well, sure" he said, "first time tracking cows for me but I'll do my best." "Ok, well thanks," said Marty, "we will get your radio set up tomorrow." With that the young officer slowly walked out to his patrol truck, not exactly sure what he was doing but clearly she wanted him out of there, so he left.

Looking out the window, "good gawd this is what they send me for a cop?" Said Ezra Jorgenson to no one there. "A puffed up boy with a new shirt on?" He answered the knock at the door, "hello I'm Officer," "I know who you are," interrupted the old man, I'm the one who called you! "Yes sir, well, you have some cows that have gone missing?" "No, they haven't gone missing, they were stolen! Dragged over the damn fence," said the old man. "Here, come out back with me, I'll show you. We've been running cows at this dairy for 50 years and have never had anything like this. Probably these damn hippies from California that have moved in around here, probably do drugs, get high at night and do all sorts of crazy ass things." "Yes sir," said Chase. "Now, here's my milking barn, here's the gate to the corral, anybody can open it, right? Easy see! If you're going to steal a cow, just open the damn gate right?" "Yes," nodded Chase. "But look, see these concrete post? We put those in twenty years ago because I was tired of replacing the busted off rail road ties we were using!" "Yes sir," said Chase. "Now see this rail," yes, "well that's four inch steel pipe, I used that to keep these damn cows from knocking down the fence and wandering off." "Occasionally we get a cougar at night, maybe a coyote, makes the cows nervous, they'll lean against the fence and bust it down, see?" "Yes sir I do," said Chase. "Well now look at this, they both walked through the cows to the back of the corral. See that, said the old man, that top rail bent down?" "Yes sir," "and look at the ground over the fence, all tore up. Something has gone on here, I'd say they used a back hoe to drag the cow over the fence and drag it off but there's no tire tracks! And to bend that rail down, that would take a lot of weight, a lot of force." "Yes it would" said Chase as he looked in wonderment. "Have you had cows stolen before?"

He asked. "Well no," said the old man. "Sometimes the gate gets left open, they wander off, not far, usually over to the hay stack or down by the road, they don't go far. That's what I don't get, they're gone, two this week, just gone, like into thin air! It's the craziest damn thing!" "Yes," said Chase, "clearly something has bent this fence down, would they have jumped? Over the fence? Scarred by lightning or something, sir?" "Oh hell kid, you're all city aren't you, dairy cows can't jump. If they went over that fence then something dragged them over that fence," said the old man.

"I guess you've read about this big cat they've got up here sir?" Asked Chase. The old man squinted and looked at him. "That's just a bunch of bull shit kid, an over sized cougar that's got everybody scarred, just a bunch of hooey. Ain't no monster cat in these parts, I've been here all my life! No cat big enough to haul off a two thousand pound cow, that's just bull shit. Damn fools, making a big deal out of nothing. Hell! Pay me! I'll get my dogs and kill your cougar. No kid, that's just BS, but my cows, they're gone and some son of a bitch has them! I want 'em back and now! I deliver to Panguitch, the creamery there, that's how I make my living, I can't go short two cows!" "No sir," replied Chase. "You don't mind if I look around a bit, out back here do you?" "Knock yourself out kid, just get my cows back," said the old man.

Chase climbed over the fence, looked at the disturbed ground, there were clear drag marks, out through the weeds toward the trees about 100 yards off. He followed the trail through the flattened brush, it was clear something large was dragged through the weeds. Once in the pine trees he could see scrapes on the bark, the floor of the forest had a trail through it. He followed for another 200 yards when he came across a paved road. On the pave road he could see large scratch marks, as if claws had dug in and slipped on the hard surface. He pulled out his phone took pictures and went to his map app, the road was the turn off to Mammoth Caves. He thought about what he had heard of this big cat in the area and a sense of fear gripped him. No, this was not BS, this was real, he had to get back and warn the farmer.

He took more pictures of the claw marks in the road and walked briskly back to the farmers house. He pounded on the door, the old man answered. "Mr. Jorgenson that big cat you've heard about is not BS, it took your cows sir, it dragged them across the road, I've got pictures of its claw marks." "Damn! You don't say son!" Said the old man, "look at that!" "Yes sir, I do say and I'm advising you to keep your cows in the barn over night, and don't go out after dark, it's not safe sir." The old man squinted his eyes and looked directly at Chase and said, "son, when you get to be my age, you don't fear nothing. I'll put my cows in the barn, but if I hear that son bitch outside, you can bet your ass I'll kill him for you. I knew that Sheriff that killed that first big cat, knew him since he was a kid, his daddy went to school with me, if Charlie Lynn's boy can kill one, well, don't you worry about me none, worry about where you're going to put that gawlt damned cow killing son bitch! Where you gonna put him in your museum!" Chase smiled at the old man's absolute confidence. "Ok Mr. Jorgenson, but please be careful, I've got to finish following those tracks, see where they lead."

Chase got in his truck and drove out on highway 14 toward the mammoth caves road, he stopped where he had earlier stood, he looked up the hill and realized the road did a series of switch backs, up to the top at the caves entrance. He decided to go to the caves and see if he could find any evidence. He noticed the drag marks entering the cave, he also saw tire tracks and foot prints over the drag marks, someone had been in the cave since the lion had been there. He took out his flash light and entered the cave, his 9mm service revolver, in his other hand. He found pieces of cow hide on the jagged rocks of the cave walls. That was enough, there was no doubt those cows were dragged into this cave. He took pictures of the cow hide and what appeared to be trails of blood, he started back out of the cave. Back at his truck he tried to call Marty on his cell, there was no service. He flipped on the emergency lights and began the drive back down the mountain to Cedar City.

"Though your sins be as scarlet."

Chapter 16

"Look! I'm not the one calling the shots here," said Marty on the phone. "The Governor's office wants results! They're not paying you to trap black bears and cougars!" Marty was losing her patients with Bob Johnson, the Montana bear trapper the Governor hired to trap what was believed to be the sole remaining South American Saber Tooth Tiger left in the world. Marty had become the de facto liaison between the governors staff and Bob. Marty and

Bob had developed a friendship during the construction and placement of the trap, old Bob had an eye for the young ladies, but that relationship was becoming strained by Bob's continued request for more money and the Governor's anger over the lack of Bob's results. Cougars and bears had been caught but the beast had not been caught! The summer tourism numbers were way down and the news cycle had moved on, the notoriety of a prehistoric predatory animal in Utah was now, yesterdays news. On top of that, a local Salt Lake gossip columnists had taken a picture of the Governor at the Grand Hotel, in a compromising embrace with a young, beautiful, female staff member. The Governor was furious, he wanted this beast caught promptly to take the media's attention off his extramarital activities, which were now becoming a story on the local nightly news. He vented his anxiety over the situation aggressively on his staff, who in turn would call Marty, in vain efforts to put more pressure on Bob to capture of the beast.

Marty was reaching the breaking point, her mentor, the Sheriff, the man she admired, the man she wanted, was dead. All around her was in chaos and there was no one to step up and take control, this temporary new Sheriff, a kid, was more interested in her and far from being capable of replacing a man like Sheriff Lynn. At 28, Chase Smith was not yet a man in Marty's eyes, a man that could take charge. She in practice, had become his boss and she was not a year out of her waitress job at the bar. The stress was building and she was starting to break down, there was nothing for her, nothing for her in this town and the pressure of her job continued to build. Her new life, her better life with the office job and the Sheriff, it was gone, it died that day with the awful news of Sheriff Jeff Lynn's death.

It was five minutes to closing, she turned over the phones, grabbed her keys and purse and headed out the door, just as she turned to lock it, she heard Chase yell from the parking lot, "Marty! Marty! Wait!" She continued to lock the door and turned to walk to her car. Chase ran up, "Marty, wait," he said, she turned and looked at him, "Marty, we've got to close Mammoth Caves, the lion is in there," he said. She responded, "Mammoth Caves is a state park, we're Iron County, we don't have jurisdiction to close it." "But we've got to!" She stopped him mid sentence and said, "deal with it. "She turned and walked to her car. She had no patience for this boy who had yet to learn to be a man.

As she pulled out of the parking lot she thought, she could not go home, not to that empty apartment again. She pulled into the parking lot of the bar where she used to work, she sat there, no, not again, she said. It's starting all over, the drinking, the men, that life, no, I can't do it, not again, I can't. She sat there, she could not go home, not to an empty apartment again. Just one drink, no more than an hour, I can't, no, just one drink, I can do that, just one and I'll go home, she promised herself.

It was two AM, the man next to her, snoring, his hairy back, his bad breath, disgusting to her. He was not a local, he said he was from Parowan, she didn't know him, it didn't matter, she was back in the hotel next to the car wash. She thought about Sheriff Lynn, how he gave her a chance and now he's gone and that chance is gone and here she is, back in the hotel, next to the car wash. She got up, went into the bathroom to clean up, searched for her clothes in the dark, got dressed and walked out. It was four blocks back to the bar where her car was still in the parking lot. She began the walk, the same path she had walked so many other nights. A patrol car pulled up next to her, no she thought, no, this can't be. It was Bill, he was on the night shift, she had arranged it for him because he needed to be with his wife during the day. "Hey" he said, "get in." She didn't respond. "Marty" he persisted, "come on, get in." She stopped, tears started rolling down her face, she got in. "Look," Bill said, "I know, it's none of my business, but come on Marty, I thought you were done with this." "Yeah, so did I, she said," through the tears. "I can't, I can't, I don't know, I just can't keep going, it's too much, with Jeff gone and all, he helped me, helped me so much, and now, I just can't." "I know" he said, "I miss him too, it's a different world without him. I don't know what the hell happened or why he had to die, it makes no sense, absolutely no sense at all." "I know" she said, "I can't understand it either, why? What happened? His wife hasn't even been in the office since he died. I don't know, it's all just so strange."

She stared and the dirty floor mats of the patrol car and said, "God I feel like shit Bill, I think I'm going to quit, move to another state, I can't stay here, I can't take it here anymore, not like this. I can't be the Sheriff's office administrator and be a weekend pick up chick at the bar." "No, you're right about that," said Bill. "But don't you think, if Jeff believed in you, enough to give you that job, that maybe you could believe in your self? Just a little?" "I don't know, it's hard, so hard," she said. "Yes it is," Bill said, "but it's hard for all of us, in different ways, all you can do is keep trying. Jeff wasn't born into that Sheriffs job, he had his issues too, you know." "I know, I know," she replied, "but he was so strong, he could handle it all." "Well, again," said Bill, "he wasn't born that way, he was 52 years old, he had some time and experience, it doesn't happen over night." She took a deep breath and responded with some anger, "I know, but I'm so alone, I have no one, men just want to fuck me, they don't love me and they never will!" "Don't say that Marty, don't say that, don't talk like that," Bill said, as he looked at the steering wheel. "I had Jeff at work," she said, "I looked forward to coming to work everyday, working with him, but now he's gone, and the only people I know, are at that bar and I just can't go home at night, alone every night, I can't live like this, there is no future for me, not here, not in this town." "I know," said Bill, "I know, but things work out, they have a way of working out, over time, they tend to work out. You will see but you have to give it time. Give it a chance, I know what happened, when we were young, I know it wasn't your fault and you got the blame, but you can't let that one thing define the rest of your life. You can't just hang out at the bar and let that be you! You know where that leads to and that's not what you want. It's not you. I remember you, from when we were young, I had a crush on you, all of us boys did. This is not you! This is not who you are!" She turned and looked at him and said, "thanks Bill, but maybe it is, maybe this is what I am." He looked down and shook his head, "no" he said, "you know it's not." She interrupted and said, "you are a good friend Bill, thank you for not judging me, thank you for trying to understand." Bill smiled and said, "well, like I said Marty, we've all got our issues, our challenges in life, we just can't give up." She looked up feigning a smile and said "thanks Bill! Jeez, look at the time, I've got to be at work in a few hours!" "Good Marty, good," he said, "be there, I'll see you there in a few."

She got out of the squad car, walked to her own car and drove home, to her apartment. She looked around, empty, like it always is. She went directly into the shower, she could not sleep, she would not sleep. Wiping the steam off the mirror, she looked into her own eyes, standing there over the sink, she looked deep. A wave of anxiety hit her, I am not who they think I am, I had Jeff fooled, I have Bill fooled, the others, but I can't fool myself, not anymore. She stood there, she started to shake, tremble, grasping the sink to hold herself up. She looked up again, how did this happen, how did I become this? When did this happen? How did this happen? I never wanted to be, I lost control somewhere, now I'm just this, bar slut, and everybody knows it and I'll never be anything else! Dark anxiety filled her heart, filled her soul. I can not get out, I can not get away from this life, from what this fucking town forces me into! I can't do it anymore, I can't!

She stepped away from the sink, gasping to catch her breath, she stumbled toward the bed, falling upon it she buried her face in the sheets, she screamed and screamed until her emotions settled into tears, sobbing. She was not in control of herself and she knew it. Her fate, her destiny, relegated to some unseen social pressure she could not escape. These people, they lie, they talk, they spread rumors and they judge. At age 32 she now recognized the image of her in this town, controlled her, was stronger than she was, it dictated how she came to be in places like that bar and in bed with dirty drunk men in cheap hotels, to be used and then discarded like trash, like the trash apparently everyone expected her to be. She had no code of ethics, no morality to follow, so she did what people expected of her. She came to the awful realization that peer pressure was her reality and she could not pretend otherwise anymore. It, controlled her, she did not control it.

Jeff helped her but now he was dead and she was back where she was when he found her, less than a year ago. It's not fair, she cried, not fair, I'm not a bad person, I'm not a bad person, I don't deserve this. She griped the bed sheets and pulled them toward her, crying, the reality of knowing she had lost control of her own life, submitted to the will of drunk men for a few extra dollars, fear and a feeling of helplessness filled her soul. The moment had arrived, her mortality, her life, was before her in this very moment and she knew it. She knew she had a choice to make.

Marty went to work that day, but spent the weekend inside, alone, drinking, considering her life, her options, she was bewildered and confused, the death of Jeff Lynn, the man who had helped her, the only man who had ever helped her, his death left a void, an uncertainty and fear. She knew the man who was vying to replace Sheriff Lynn, she had been with him when she was young, much too young. She could not bear the thought of him becoming sheriff. At the time, she was 16, he was 25 and married, but he would not let her be, until one night at the park, he had his way with her, and everyone in town knew it, including his wife. They eventually divorced and he remarried, but it was always considered to be Marty's fault, the break up of his first marriage, she was the little sixteen year old slut home wrecker as the people in town saw her. She never lived down that reputation. Her father, a drunk, gave her a beating when he found out and she left the house, never to return. She lived with several different men, eventually marrying one who said he loved her, only to catch him with her friend. She had lost all respect for herself by that time and then Sheriff Lynn and his officers raided the bar that night less than a year ago, instead of arresting her, he gave her a chance, a job and a chance at a new life. He knew she had been wrongfully accused, wrongfully judged and he wanted to correct that. But that chance was over now, with Sheriff Lynn dead and a new sheriff coming in, a new Sheriff she could not bear to be in the same room with.

It was Sunday morning, she was hung over, head pounding and she needed air. Rolling off the bed and into the bathroom, the mirror was not kind. She yanked a brush through what was once, beautiful, soft, radiant hair. Pulled on her worn jeans, slipped into a hooded sweat shirt, tennis shoes, and stumbled down the stairs. The sidewalk, cold and hard, but it was there, she could depend upon it. It was built by someone a long time ago, someone now dead and buried in the ground, someone she would never know, but that persons work, was there, for her, here and now and she was grateful for it. In this moment of crisis, she would walk and this, she could do, walk on this sidewalk to get away, anywhere but here, anywhere but this. On this lonely Sunday morning, reality crashing down with each passing sound, she was grateful for that sidewalk, it was real and something she could depend upon, unlike everyone and everything else, in her life, in this small cruel town.

It was still early, the cool of the morning felt harsh but good, an awakening to reality. It was quiet, peaceful. She saw children dressed in their Sunday best, running to church. On the side walk, she could hear faint singing, she looked up and saw the church in the bleary distance. As she approached she heard hymns being sung. The words became clear. The words had meaning, like the sidewalk she was on, they had always been there, she remembered them from her childhood. The words were sung by the congregation, as if sung to her. These words she knew and now, they meant so much, "I'll strengthen thee, help thee and cause thee to stand."

She stood there on that sidewalk and smiled, looking into the morning sun and the distant church. She walked to it, turned and walked in. She knew she was a mess but didn't care, this was her life, here and now, she had no pretenses and felt no need, she was what she was, and she wanted to be in this church. Looking around as people sang, she sat down in the back row just as the hymn ended and the prayer was given. Bowing her head, she felt warmth, acceptance, peace, not fear, not judgment.   She felt comfort as the prayer went on, the person prayed that we all might be more understanding and forgiving of one another. Tears started streaming down her cheek before the prayer was over.

As she looked up, she noticed an older woman sitting nearby, she looked familiar, then she realized it was Mrs. Warren, Carl Warren's widow, who came in the office to thank Sheriff Lynn for being so kind after her husband had been killed on the mountain. They exchanged smiles in this brief moment, this brief moment of acceptance, Marty felt like she would stay. It felt good to be here, in this church it was peaceful, there was a place to be. She would stay and hear the talk given on the atonement of Christ and the forgiveness and peace it brings. In her heart she felt something, a purity she had not felt since she had been in church as a little girl. This felt like coming home.

Just leave me alone

Chapter 17

Christine Lynn starred at the computer screen, reading her state benefits report. She was perplexed, it said she should be receiving Jeff's social security death benefits, she didn't know that she was. Outside she heard men talking, close to her house. Her computer went off, she checked the power button, looking up, the clock was off, she stood up and flipped the light switch, nothing. She heard the metal clank that sounded like the multi breaker box closing. She looked out the closed front drapes, it was a city truck, in front of her house, she saw two men walking from her backyard. She stepped out on the porch, and looked at the men, they stopped. She said, "did the power go off?" "Yes," they said, "we shut it off." "Why?" she said. "Because you didn't pay your bill!" "Oh!" She thought for a moment. The man asked her, "do you have money to pay the bill?" "Well yes," she said. "Well, you need to go down to the city, pay the bill and we will come back and turn on your power." "Can't I just pay you," she asked? "No, we can't take money, but we will be out here for a few more hours, if you can get it paid we can turn it back on today." "Well, alright" she said, "but I think you could have told me first." He turned and looked, the shut off notice was hanging on her door. It had been there for the statutory minimum of three days. The man smiled and walked to his truck.

Christine walked back into her house, it was near noon and she was still in her robe. She hurried to get dressed and drive downtown to get her power turned back on. Standing in line she was oblivious to those around her. "Ma'am? Ma'am" the clerk said. "Oh, yes" answered Christine, "they turned my power off, I guess I forgot to pay the bill." "Yes," said the clerk, "well let's get this taken care of and get your power back on."

The road back home passed by the cemetery. Christine felt repelled by the place, like some force was pushing her away from it. She took a breath and turned into the cemetery drive way. Walking out to Jeff's grave, she didn't know why she was here, what she was doing, only that she was going to the grave of her once husband. It was still dirt, the sod had not been replaced, a temporary marker, no headstone yet. She stood there, looking at the grave. Why? Why didn't you just kill me and take me with you? Why did you lie to me, why did you cheat on me, why did you commit adultery? Why? And then die like a coward! A god damned coward, leaving me here to suffer! Why? She spit on the grave, kicked the dirt, then fell to her knees and laid on the grave, she wanted her man back, her former life back, more than she wanted anything, she did not want to live, not now, not like this, take me you son of a bitch! Take me, she said, face in the dirt! Why did you leave me here? Why? What did I do to deserve this? She rose to her hands and knees, tears dropping on the dry dirt, sobbing and gasping for breath, she tried to collect herself, and walked back to her car. There was nothing, no reason to be here, no reason to live. She pulled into her driveway, walking into the house, the power not on yet, she walked into the bedroom, laid on the bed. This dark, cold, stale existence, it was not going to change, and the realization of that hit her like a punch in the gut, she gasped for breath, no, this was not going to change. He left her here and it was not going to change. The terror of that thought gripped her heart, living life like this was a fate worse than death. Jeff got out easy, she was left here, by him, he left her here, alone, to suffer.

She heard the refrigerator start up in the kitchen, the power was back on. Her sister had tried to call several times, but her cell phone was dead, it had not been plugged in for several days. The door bell rang, she ignored it, then someone started pounding on the door, still, she ignored it. Then she heard keys, and the door unlock. It was her sister, she walked into the bedroom! "What are you doing? You don't answer your phone? For days? You don't answer the door? What are you doing?" The sister demanded an answer. The quiet response was, "just leave me alone." "No! I will not" yelled the sister. "Why don't you answer my calls?" Christine turned away and repeated, "just leave me alone." "No! Mrs. Halverson called and said she saw the utility workers turning off your power? Why?" "I forgot to pay the bill," said Christine. "What do you mean you forgot? The notice is on your door!" "I didn't see it," she said. "You didn't see it? When was the last time you were out of the house? Why are you all dirty?" "Just leave me alone Ann, please, just leave me alone." "No! We're getting out of this house! You're not going to live like this! Get showered, get dressed, we're getting out of here!" "No, just leave me alone." At which point Ann grabbed Christine's arm and Christine threw back violently out of Ann's grasp. Sitting up on the end of the bed she yelled! "Now get out! Get out! Now!"   Ann stepped back to the wall and stared at her sister. "You don't understand, and you'll never understand, so just get out and leave me alone." Ann stood there staring. "Go back to your shitty little life Ann, your boring husband, your flunky kids, take your crap life and go!" Yelled Christine! "This is out of your league! You don't know! And you'll never know! So just get out!"

Ann, stunned, stood there, staring at Christine in silence, never had she seen her sister act like this, this was not the person she had known all her life.

"Well," she finally said, "this is not how family acts!"
"No," replied Christine, "it's not, I'm not your family, not anymore, now get out or I'll call the cops!" Yelled Christine. Ann took two steps and stopped, she took Christine's house key off her key ring and threw it on the floor, then stormed out the front door.

Christine sat there, staring at the wall. She laid back down and starred at the ceiling. There was nothing, just this loud pain, this deafening roar of awful silence. She thought of Jeff, she longed for his closeness, yet at the same time, she knew he had been with that other woman. The thing she longed for was the thing she hated more than anything she had ever hated in her life, exponentially more than she had ever imagined she could hate someone, a hatred that she did not know she was capable of, and yet, still, she loved him. The incongruity crippled her, it was like a cramp, a painful cramp that would not ease but grew stronger day after day.

The hours passed, it was now well after dark. Christine got up, walked out side and started walking, she didn't know where, she didn't pay attention, she just kept walking. After two hours she was on a dirt road, west of town, staring blankly ahead as she walked. She could think of nothing but Jeff, in that grave, the cruelty of his death, the insult to the injury he had inflicted. Walking on, blindly staring forward into the dark, the image of Jeff's grave fixed in her mind, suddenly she became aware of a loud sound, a roaring sound. She had walked up upon a rail road crossing, the freight train was traveling south at 70 miles an hour. She stopped, staring at it for a moment before she comprehended what it was. Without thinking further, she walked forward into the path of the train. She walked into the side of the passing rail cars, the force threw her forward, her frail body flying 20 feet onto the jagged broken rocks used as a base for the rail road tracks. Her forearm badly gashed, her head cut and bleeding, she remained conscious and aware of the loud noise next to her head, the wheels of the train were not two feet from her head, passing at 70 mph. She laid there stunned as the train passed. Slowly she became aware that she was hurt, laying on sharp rocks on the embankment of the side of the rail road tracks. She struggled to get to her hands and feet. It was dark and it was cold, but it was a full moon, and the pain of the wounds were becoming very real and very intense, her head, throbbing. She got to her feet, climbed back up the embankment and walked to the edge of the road where she fell back down and rolled to a sitting position on the dirt road. She became aware of something warm, in her lap, on her legs, it was slippery, in the moon light she could see it was blood flowing from her arm, a three inch gash in her lower forearm. She sat there, unaware of anything other than the cold, the moon and the blood flowing out of her arm onto her leg and on to the dirt road.

Chad Peterson threw a shovel in the back of his truck, he had several canvas dams to set to turn his water. His water share was turned into his ditch this night at 3am, he had to divert it onto his grain with a canvas dam at the south end of his field. He drove 40 mph down the dirt road, not yet fully awake, he approached the rail road crossing, the truck nearly leaving the ground as he crossed it. There was something in the road, he threw the wheel hard to the left to miss it, the truck swapped a couple times on the dirt road before it corrected itself. Damn he thought, what the hell was that? He slammed on the brakes, looking back in the red of his brake lights, there was something there in the road. He threw it into reverse, getting out, he saw it was a person, an older lady, bloody, dirty and cut up, a gash on her head, sitting in a pool of blood. What the hell he said. "Lady! What are you doing? Are you alive?" She was unresponsive. "Come on, get up, we've got to get you to the doctor." He reached to lift her and she groaned, resisted his grasp. "Come on lady we've got to go." He stepped around behind her, grabbed her under her arms and easily lifted her into the front seat of his truck. She was light, much lighter than the hay bails he regularly threw on his truck. He slammed the door shut and yelled, "stay there!" Running around to the drivers side he jumped in, put the Ford in drive and raced toward the hospital emergency room.

A gurney was brought out, Christine was now unconscious, she was wheeled directly into an examination room where a team of nurses and a doctor went to work on her immediately. The admittance nurse asked Chad to come to her desk, she began asking him questions about the woman he brought in. The police were already on their way, she had called them when she saw the woman on the gurney. Chad knew nothing other than he found her near the train tracks on county road 4. Officer Bill Stevens of the Sheriffs office arrived. He joined the interrogation of Chad. Chad was starting to wonder if he was being accused when Bill asked the nurse, "can I see her?" She looked at her computer, the patient was still in the examination room receiving a blood transfusion, "yes, if you'll walk with me please." Bill turned to Chad and said, "sit tight!" "Am I being arrested?" Asked Chad? "No, just stay for a minute will you?" "Of course," said Chad. "I didn't do anything wrong!"

The nurse walked with Bill to the examination room, she pulled back the curtain. "My God!" Said Bill. "That's Christine Lynn, my bosses wife! My former boss!" "Sheriff Lynn?" Asked the nurse? "His wife?" "Yes!" He said. "What happened? What is she doing here?" The blood transfusion had brought Christine back to a state of semi consciousness. She looked up at Bill and recognized him. He asked her, "can we talk?" The doctor turned and said in anger, "get him out of here, she's not out of the woods yet." Christine blankly starred at Bill, he stepped back, letting the curtain close.

"God, what has happened to that family, they are good people, first Jeff now this. I just don't understand it, I just don't," said Bill. They walked back to the admittance desk where Chad was still waiting. "Tell me again, how you found her, Chad?" Asked Bill. "I told you, I came over the rail road tracks and there she was, sitting in the road. Lucky I didn't hit her." "And why were you out there at 3 in the morning?" "I told you, I was changing the water on my grain," said Chad. "Gawd! I can see why people don't help anybody anymore, they get accused!" Said Chad. "You're not accused," said Bill. "It's just impossible to understand how Sheriff Lynn's widow ends up bloody and beat up on a road five miles outside of town in the middle of the night! Like she was dumped there!" Said Bill. "That's Sheriff Lynn's wife?" Asked a bewildered Chad. "Yes," said Bill, "it is, I shouldn't have told you that but it is."

"I saw the shovel and canvas dams in the back of your truck on my way in," said Bill. "Your story checks out, so you can go, but we may be in touch again, please don't leave town without letting us know. You don't want a search warrant out on you right?"Asked Bill. "Oh, no, absolutely not, I didn't do anything, all I wanted to do was help,"said Chad. "You did" said Bill, "you might have saved her life. She'd of probably bled out had you not come along." Chad nodded in agreement. He got up and walked out to his truck which was still at the emergency entrance. The sun was just coming up. Bill looked at the admitting nurse and shook his head. "I don't know what's happening, it's just like things have gone completely crazy since that damn cat was found on the mountain. It's just so damn bizarre." "I heard about that," said the nurse. "They say there is another one, is that true?" She asked. "I'm afraid it is," said Bill, "god damned afraid it is true." He shook his head, got up and walked out of the hospital toward his patrol car. He drove back to the office and waited for Marty to arrive.

Marty walked in, wearing tight jeans and a Henley shirt, she wasn't trying to be sexy but she was, she couldn't help it, these were the only kind of clothes she had, what she wore working at the bar. Bill thought to himself, she's still dressing like a hussy, somebody needs to get ahold of this woman, she can't go on living like this. He thought he might say something but then he realized, he shouldn't.

"Good morning Bill," said Marty as she walked in. Bill responded by saying, "Christine Lynn is in the hospital." Shocked, Marty turned and asked "why? What happened?" "I don't know Bill said, she was found out on county road 4, next to the rail road tracks, all bloody and beat up. They had to give her transfusions, she was nearly bled out." "Oh my god!" Said Marty. "Is she going to be alright?" "I don't know" Bill said, "she took a pretty nasty hit to the head, they're keeping her in the ICU at the hospital." "I should go to her," said Marty. "No" said Bill, "they won't let you see her." Marty shook her head, "what next?" She asked. "That is so terrible, what is next!" "I know," said Bill, "a widow, an older woman like that, beat up, dumped out on that road in the middle of the night, things have just gone crazy around here, I don't know what it is, but this town ain't the same anymore. Something has changed, and I don't know what it is." He looked up at Marty and said, "somebody should go out to her house, investigate it as a crime scene. Something is amiss here, Christine is not the kind of person this happens to. Somebody might be thinking they'll get retaliation on Sheriff Lynn's widow, now that he's gone, punish her for Jeff arresting them or something, who knows, with all these psychos in the world. I don't know, but something isn't right about this. We need to do a crime scene investigation out there." Just then Chase Smith walked in, smiled and nodded his head and walked into Sheriff Lynn's office. "Who is that?"

Asked Bill. "Oh, that's Sheriff Chase Smith, Salt Lake sent him down here to fill in for Sherif Lynn until the county replaces him." "Oh," said Bill, "so he's my new boss?" "No" said Marty, "he's just a kid, 28, college grad, I'll send him out to Christine's house." "Well, I better go out there with him then!" "No," said Marty, "you're off the clock!" "I know" said Bill, "but this is too important." Marty called Chase over the intercom, "can you come out here?" "Yes" he replied. The two men met in front of Marty's desk, discussed the situation and drove out to Christine's house in Bill's patrol car.

The door was wide open when the two officers arrived at Christine's house. They walked in, finding nothing amiss they moved through the other rooms. On the floor of the master bedroom was a key, it was bagged as evidence to be sent to the crime lab in Salt Lake. Further searching found nothing wrong. Bill looked across the street, he saw an older woman watching them from her front doorstep.

He walked across the street and said "hello, I'm Officer Bill Stevens with the county Sheriffs office, can I ask you a few questions?" "Well certainly" she said, "I'm always willing to help the police." "What is your name," he asked. "I'm Patricia Halverson, I've been the Lynn's neighbor for 30 years." "Yes," he said, "did you see anything suspicious or unusual in the past couple days?" "Well yes," she said, "the fact that you are here! Where is Christine, why is her door open?" "That's what we're trying to find out Ma'am. Did you see anyone at the house lately?" "Yes, Ann Folger, Christine's sister. I called her because the power company came out and shut off Christine's power, I wanted to make sure she was ok. I knocked but no one answered, so I called her sister." "About what time did you see her sister arrive?" He asked. "That was about noon yesterday." "Did you notice anything unusual about her visit, did she leave in a hurry?" "Well, yes she did. They had a fight! A terrible fight, I could hear them arguing from here, she left the front door open when she went in, I could hear them fighting, it was awful." "Did she open the door or did Christine let her in?" He asked. "No, she opened the door, I saw that, Christine did not come to the door." "What we're they arguing about? Could you hear them?" "I don't know, but I could hear Christine yelling at her sister very loud, She was saying, or screaming, to get out, leave her alone, that I heard, very loud, you couldn't mistake it." "Did she leave her alone?"Asked Bill? "Well, I saw her leave, when she left she slammed the door so hard I could hear it from here! Then she gave me a dirty look as she walked to her car. We're not friends, but we've been acquainted for years, she has no call to be angry with me." "I see" said Bill. "So she left here angry?" "Oh yes," said Mrs Halverson, "no question about that." "Did you see her come back? Anytime later?" Asked Bill. "No, I didn't, but we go to bed around nine, so anything after that, I wouldn't know about, but I saw the door open early this morning around six, then you arrived."

"Ok, well thank you Mrs. Halverson, we may be in touch later." "Well, where is Christine? She asked?" "I can't say right now Mrs. Halverson," said Bill as he walked toward the patrol car. Opening the trunk, Bill looked up at Chase and said, "lock the place up, put stickers on the doors, time mark them, this is an active crime scene. I think we know what happened to Christine."

The Slaughter House

Chapter 18

"Iron County Sheriffs office, Marty speaking, how can I help you?" "Uh, yeah, we need somebody up here, there's cows on the highway." "Ok, well who are you and where are you," asked Marty. "Oh, sorry," said the caller, "I'm Chantel and I work at the Quik Stop on the corner of Highway 89 and 14 in Todd's Junction. There's cows in our parking lot and they're wandering out on 89, ones going to get hit by a car." "How many cows?" Marty asked. "I can count, six from here, and they're not range cows, they're big cows, like dairy cows," said the caller. "Ok we will get somebody up there,"said Marty. "Base to four," called Marty, "this is four go ahead." "Joe, we've got some loose cows on the highway up by the Quik Stop in Todd's Junction, can you respond?" "Yes, how many cows," asked Joe. "The caller said six was all she could see from inside the gas station, she said they were wandering out on 89, she also said they were dairy cows."

Hearing this over the radio Chase interrupted, "5 to base!" "Go ahead" said Marty. "That's got to be Mr. Jorgenson's cows, he's the guy that called in a few days ago, missing two dairy cows, I spoke with him, he's got a dairy up there." "Can you call him," asked Marty. "Yes, give me a minute" replied, Chase. "He's not answering, I can respond to this," "ok" said Marty. Joe responded, "six dairy cows, you're going to need a trailer, I'll call Hafen's and see if they can send somebody up with their trailer." "Thank you" replied Chase.

Chase pulled into the dirt drive way leading to Mr. Jorgenson's farm, he noticed two cows feeding on the front lawn, this is not good he thought. There was no response to his knocks on the door, he walked out back and toward the milking barn and corral. Nothing seemed amiss, then he glanced over to the large red barn some 75 yards in the distance. He could see right away, there were no doors on the barn, as he walked closer he saw the doors laying in the dirt, looking up on the barn he could see where the hinges had been ripped apart, a shotgun laying on the ground at the entrance to the barn. Fear gripped his body, his shoulders tightened as he walked inside the barn, to his left, a dead cow, it's throat ripped out, further back another dead cow, nearly severed in half at the mid spine. Back to the right, the disemboweled body of Mr Jorgenson, against the wall, thrown there from 30 feet away at the door, four large claw marks across his mid section, his entrails exposed and laying in the dirt, his eyes wide open in the stunned, blank, terrified stare of a dead man.

Chase felt a wave of nausea come over him, panic and trembling, he grabbed his hand held radio, "Marty" he called, "Marty, Marty!" "Yes," she replied, "who is this?" "Ah, this, is, Chase, I, I, I need help!" "Chase what is the matter," she asked. "He's dead," said Chase, "that lion got him, that lion got in the barn, it killed him and some cows, I need help." "Who is dead?" asked Marty. "Mr. Jorgenson, he's dead," said Chase. "I told him, I told him to put the cows in the barn and he did and now he's dead." "Hold on," Marty said, "I'll get someone up there." Just then Officer Joe Woodard interrupted, "base this is four, call the forensics team out of Salt Lake, get them up there ASAP, I'm on my way, four out!" Joe threw on his siren and lights and drove as fast as he could up the twisty mountain road that was Highway 14.

As Joe drove in the Jorgenson's dairy he saw Chase sitting in his car. "What are you doing," asked Joe. "I can't go back in there," said Chase. "Yes you can," said Joe, "you are the acting Sheriff, you have to go back in there." "No, please," said Chase, "I've never seen a dead man before, I can't do it if this is the job, I just can't." "Yes you can Chase, we all have to deal with this, sooner or later. Today is that day for you, come on, I'll walk you through it." Chase got up and looked at Joe, Chase's hands were shaking, sweat beading on his face, he was pale. Joe said, "come on, get some air in your lungs, you write the report, I'll dictate it to you."

As they approached the barn door, Joe picked up four shotgun shells on the ground, "double ought buck and deer slugs," he said, "if the old man hit anything, it'll have some big holes in it!" Walking in they saw the cows then turned to the right and walked up to the body of Mr. Jorgenson. "Gawd damn!" said Joe! "Look at that!" "I can't" said Chase, "four claw marks, his rib cage is ripped out, that cat threw him from the door with one swipe of its paw, that's got to be 30 feet! Damn," said Joe, "I heard this cat was big but what could do this to a 200 pound man?" He stood back and took pictures. Walking over to the cows, "this one looks like the cat had it by the throat, this other one, it's spine is ripped right in half, I'd bet the cat had the first cow by the throat when the old man came in blasting away, the cat ran back, this cow got in the way, he ripped it in half with his paw, then turned on the old man when he ran out of shells." Chase didn't say a word, he just nodded his head. "The cows out front, the ones at the gas station, just ran out after it was all over. That's what we've got here Chase." Again, Chase just nodded his head. "Look" said Joe, "why don't you run down to the gas station and see if you can keep the cows off the highway until Hafen gets here." "Thanks Joe," said Chase. "I know kid, I know, but you'll get used to it, we see dead people, it's just part of the job." "Ok," said Chase. "When I was here before, I found the trail where the lion dragged the cows, it's just out back past the fence. Cat might have gone back the same way, he drags them into Mammoth Cave." "Thanks Chase, I'll check it out," said Joe.

Joe walked out of the barn, looked at the barn doors laying on the ground, he looked at the twisted metal that used to be the hinges. "Damn!" He said, out loud, "that's quarter inch steel!" He looked to his right and saw the fence Chase had mentioned, looking down he could see a drag trail with a steady stream of dried blood leading to the fence, where the steel rail had been bent down to the lower rail. Climbing over the fence, he had second thoughts about proceeding into the brush and trees, he chambered a shell into his 9mm service weapon and walked toward the tree line. Just at the tree line he found what he was looking for, a dead cow with a huge lion, nearly the same size as the cow, still locked on the cows neck. Joe stepped back, he could see the holes where Jorgenson had emptied his shotgun into the side of the cat, blood and tissue around the holes. He stared at the scene, like something out of prehistoric Africa he thought, hard to believe he was seeing what was before him. He grabbed his hand held radio and called Marty.

The following day the University Zoology department's investigation team arrived, State Wild Life Department, the forensics team from Salt Lake County and a whole host of other state and federal agencies. Three helicopters were in the parking lot of the Quik Stop gas station. The body of the lion was strapped into a sling and airlifted on to the back of a flat bed truck and then transferred into a refrigerated truck and shipped to Salt Lake. An ambulance carried the body of Mr. Jorgenson to Cedar City where it was identified by one of his adult sons. He was hailed as a hero in the local paper for having killed what was thought to be the last remaining lion on the mountain.

The forensics team later explored the cave where they found the partial remains of the missing couple from Brianhead and Professor Dreyfus. The official position of the State of Utah and national media outlets was that the lions were the result of an illegal cloning experiment arranged for a Las Vegas entertainment show. It was said that they broke out of their cages and made their way into the wilds of the central mountains of Utah. The scientist of the University of Utah and others that studied the cats, strongly disagreed but they were told by both state and federal agencies, in no uncertain terms, to keep their opinions to themselves, or they would lose their state and federal grants. The bodies of the cats were taken by the Federal Department of the Interior and allegedly stored for further study, though the University of a Utah and all others that wanted access, were denied.

The girls camp reopened, Brianhead ski resort remained open with no further problems. A sheep herder who ranged his sheep on Cedar Mountain complained to the Department of Wild Life that he was loosing far too many sheep to predation over the summer, the response was that there was a very healthy cougar population on the mountain. Similar complaints came in from ranchers about missing cattle and horses, they received the same reply. Every state agency was told to kill the story, eliminate it from their data bases, do not talk of it to anyone for any purpose. The State of Utah wanted to forever erase any memory of the prehistoric cats that were on the mountain that summer.

A married couple from Las Vegas were enjoying their beautiful new cabin in Right Hand Canyon on Cedar Mountain. They were enjoying the view of the sunset as they had dinner on their cliff side deck. The cool of the evening was just descending as the sun was setting. They began taking a video of the beautiful moment when a deafening blast of hissing air came out of nowhere, it was followed by a loud deep throated growl. Primal fear pierced their soul, they ran inside the cabin. Never had they heard anything like that, they were literally shaking inside their new beautiful summer retreat. There was little discussion, they did not stop to gather things. The garage was in the basement, they ran downstairs to their car and back to Las Vegas that night.

At home, days later, their 16 year old daughter watched the video and posted it on YouTube. It received well over a million views and several hundred comments about the lions that had killed people on Cedar Mountain the summer before. It started an online debate about the validity of the lions and whether more could still exist. The legend of the Cedar Mountain Saber Tooth Tiger would not die. The couple listed their cabin for sale and never returned to Right Hand Canyon on Cedar Mountain.

This is What Hell is

Chapter 19

It was 7:30am Sunday morning and Rachel Stewart sat in the church leadership counsel meeting, stiff and ridged, like a spring waiting to explode. The Sunday School teacher sitting next to her could feel the tension and stress radiating from her. She had returned to her husband and daughter, but for nearly a year now, she had kept what she had done, to herself. She was silent in the meeting, taking notes but offering little. Bishop Wayne Ryan and others in the church leadership had noticed a change in her over the past several months. Her demeanor had changed, she was too quiet at times, too loud at others, seemed detached, her mind somewhere else, struggling to be what she had always been, but now, she could not be.

The meeting broke and each member went to their specific area of the chapel to prepare for the days classes at church. Rachel went back to the Women's room and sat alone, in silence, staring at the wall. She could hear the organ music in the chapel start, she took a deep breath and walked out into the hallway toward the main chapel for the start of Sunday services. Familiar people greeted her, she forced a smile but did not stop to talk. She sat in her usual spot, alone, her husband and daughter joined her shortly before the meeting began. The opening prayer was given, the songs sung and the sacrament administered. She knew she was not worthy to partake of the sacred sacrament ordinance but she did, in an intense moment of forcing her own rationalization, upon the sacred ordinance of the church. Her hand shook, spilling the sacrament water, her husband looking on at her, in bewilderment, his wife, in obvious decline. She knew she was starting to come apart. She knew people were noticing, still, the situation forced her hand, forced her masquerade. She could not reveal her guilt, her anguish and remorse but neither could she hide it any longer. She decided, she could not go on further, she had to confide in someone, the weight of her sin was exposing her facade, cracking her hardened polished veneer, the reality of her phony life, was becoming exposed.

After the service came to a close the Bishop was greeting people as they left the chapel, she grabbed his arm as she walked by, "I need to see you!" "Oh! Well! Sister Stewart," the Bishop responded in startled reply, "I've got appointments, Brother Whipple is in his office, check with him, I'm sure he can get you in sometime later today." "No!" She said firmly, "Now! Not later, now, it has to be now!" He furrowed his brow, looked into the eyes of the woman who had sat on his Bishop's Counsel for years, worked with him for years, he turned and looked at those waiting to see him, several elderly women sat waiting in the hallway, two young boys waiting for their advancement interviews, he looked back at her and saw in her eyes a desperation he had not seen before, and he said, "just a moment." He walked into his clerks office, "can you reschedule my first hour?" "Well, yes," said Brother Whipple, with a bewildered look on his face. "It's necessary or I wouldn't ask," said the Bishop.

She sat in the chair directly in front of the Bishop's desk, a chair she had stepped past many times before, now she was in it, the chair where the sins of the ward, the community that she had belonged to for so many years, where the sins of her community were confessed. "Well, what is it" asked the Bishop, in a slightly annoyed voice, annoyed that one of his leadership members was apparently, about to fail him. She said nothing, tears started rolling down her face, he handed her a tissue, her make up running. "I can't," she said, "this was a mistake, I'm sorry," she started to get up. "No," he said, "obviously it's something, you need to stay," he said, "we can't carry the weight," she interrupted him mid sentence and said, "I've committed adultery."

He looked down at his desk then looked up. "With who? Someone in the ward?" "No," she said, "no one you know." "Well," said the Bishop, "I can't tell you how sorry I am to hear this, have you told your husband?" "No, I can't, that's why I'm here, to confess to you, I can't tell him." "Well, you've taken the first step, you've come here to confess before God and as you well know, God requires us to confess to those we've sinned against, those we've harmed with our actions. Adultery is a very serious sin, a sin against God, a sin against the church, against the family and perhaps worst of all, a sin against ourselves, but there is a way back, and full confession is the beginning of that way back. You must confess to your husband." "No! I can't," she said adamantly, "don't you understand," she yelled back at him.

He looked at her, she looked down, there's more, she said, people are dead, and it's my fault. Taken aback, the Bishop looked at her intently. What do you mean people are dead? "He is dead," she said, "him and his wife." "Who is dead?" He asked. "The man I had sex with! He died! I can't, I can't say who it is right now," she said, shaking her head. "But he was a good man, a great man, but something happened and he died, I think he killed himself, in his truck, I think he intentionally killed himself in a crash."

The Bishop paused for a moment, "is this that Sheriff up in Cedar City? The one that saved our group at girls camp?" Asked the Bishop. She looked down, she knew she had said too much. She shook her head, "I don't know why, I don't know why he did that, I don't know why, he knew I loved him, he knew that! I told him! He felt it, he knew it, I know he did! I don't know why he died but I know it wasn't an accident, that man would not die like that, not that way, not like that. He did it and I think he did it because of me." "Why because of you?" The Bishop asked. "Because of what we did, she said. I don't know, it makes no sense. He said he loved his wife, that we should separate for a while, and then he was dead, I don't know why, it makes no sense, no sense at all."

"And his wife?" The Bishop asked. "She died, she just died in the hospital, somebody beat her and she died. Oh God it's awful, I don't know why, I don't know why but I know it's my fault, somehow it's my fault! Oh dear God! What did I do, what did I do!" "Just, just, slow down," the Bishop said. "How do you know somebody beat her?" "Because that's what the secretary said, the secretary at the Sheriffs office. She was found on a road, his wife, all beaten up like somebody dumped her there, then she died, in the hospital, she just died! Oh God, I can't bear it anymore. It's because of me, it's because I loved him, I loved him that night, that night at the camp, I know it, somehow I know it, he killed himself because of me and what we did. His wife knew, I know she knew! They said it was the truck, in the news, they said there was something wrong with the truck," she said. "There was nothing wrong with the truck, he used that truck to save us, he pulled the tree out of the road with that truck, there was nothing wrong with it! He did it himself, he did it himself!"

"Why," the Bishop asked. "Why?" "I don't know why," she cried. "I didn't say a thing to his wife, but she knew, I could tell she knew, and then that body, Bob, Bob's corpse, in that trailer, she saw it and she started screaming at him, in front of everybody and then she left and I knew, and he knew. It was horrible. Horrible! And then, he wouldn't look at me, we just, got the kids out of there but he wouldn't look at me. I knew it was bad then, I knew it was bad. But I loved him, he knew that, I loved him, he had to know that! I did, I loved him! I've never loved a man like that, never like that, it was real Bishop, don't you see, it was real! For the first time in my life, it was real! But then he was dead, and, I saw it on the news. And there was nothing that I could do! Nothing! I didn't know he'd kill himself! I didn't know! Nothing ever said or suggested to me, nothing made me think, that a man like that, a strong man, a brave man, would take his own life. Nothing, there was nothing, and now he's dead! I still can't believe it. I mean, he went out there in the dark, with that beast and he killed it, by himself, he killed it! And then, the news said he was dead, it makes no sense, no sense at all."

The Bishop looked down, "have you told the police in Cedar City?" He asked. "No, she said, they're looking for the person that killed his wife. If they knew this they would suspect me!" "Did you kill her?" The Bishop bluntly asked. She looked up through her tears, aghast, and said, "how can you ask me that? How can you even think that?" He looked back at her, "adultery is a very serious sin, it inflames serious passions, murder is often associated with adultery. I'll ask you again, did you kill her?" "No!" She responded in a raised voice.

He took a deep breath as he continued to stare at her, well, "I believe you," he said, "but this is a very serious matter. I may have to go to the police about this." "No! No! You can't, it would destroy my daughter, for her to know I was involved in this!" "Well, good thing she wasn't at the camp but this is going to come out! She will eventually know!" Said the Bishop. "No! No she won't!" Rachel rose out of her chair and smashed her fist down on his desk! "No she won't! I'll sue you if any of this leaves this office! Do you understand me? Do you understand me Wayne! Do you hear? I'll sue!" She yelled.

The Bishop looked up at her, silent, now knowing the dilemma before him was serious not only for her, but for him and his family as well. He looked down and shook his head, "Rachel, Rachel!" He said, "what have you got yourself into?" She responded, "look, I know for me, my life is over, but not for my daughter, not for her, do you understand that, whatever comes out of this, not for my daughter!" The Bishop looked at her, "I can't undo what you've done Rachel, I can't, it's not just you that suffers Rachel, it's not just you. That's why adultery is so serious!" He said. "Not my daughter!" She yelled!

There was a knock on the door. The ward clerk, Brother Whipple, stuck his head in the door, "is everything alright" he asked? The Bishop looked up, "cancel the rest of my day, send everyone home, we're done for the day." Brother Whipple stood there, "please, just do it," said the Bishop. The door closed, he turned his head back to Rachel. "Look," he said, "if you've committed a crime, a serious crime, I have to report it, that's in our handbook, I have to, that's the rule." "I haven't she said, I didn't kill his wife! I didn't do it! I was here, in Las Vegas, I didn't do it! Look! Look, here, my reservation at the Bellagio, I wasn't in Cedar City!" She held up her phone which still had the reservation on it. "I didn't even know until I went there to talk to her!" He took a deep breath, "why were you going to talk to her?" "Because I knew she knew, because I felt responsible for his death, because I knew she had lost her husband and it was my fault! Because I felt terrible, because I knew it was my fault!"

The Bishop shook his head, "ok, but I need to speak to the Stake President about this, this is a matter for the Stake President." "No! Not a word! Do you understand me! Not a word, priest/penitent privilege! I'm invoking that Wayne! Do you understand me? I'm invoking that! Do you understand what that means?" "Yes, of course," the Bishop said, "but we have a limited privilege in our rules." "Not in the law you don't! Not in the law!" Yelled Rachel.

The Bishop thought about it for a moment, "ok" he said, "OK! The law is not my concern, your soul is my concern, your husband, your family, these are my concerns." She looked at him, "they must not know! They can't know. My husband will divorce me, he will take my daughter, she will not survive that, she'll turn to drugs, she's already so unhappy, unhappy with me, with her father, we've had her in counseling, she's struggling, I can't put her through this!" "I'm afraid she's already in it Rachel, kids have a way of sensing things," the Bishop said.

She looked down, "oh God, it was only a moment, only a moment, and that thing, that lion was out there, I needed that man, I needed him, you don't understand, that night, you don't understand." "No, I don't," said the Bishop, "I don't know how adultery has anything to do with our young women's camp! All I know is that man was a hero in my mind, until a few moments ago." "Oh, he was a hero Bishop, if you only knew, he was the only one, the only one, he went out there in that awful night and he killed it. Without him, I don't know what would have happened, we may have all died, we needed him, your daughter was there, she needed him, without him I don't know what would have happened. Don't destroy his name by letting this get out. You owe him that, you owe me that, I was there, I helped him, we helped your daughter! Don't do this!"

He looked at her, still perplexed at how she was involved and how all of this had unfolded. "Ok, well look, obviously you can't hold your church position, with all of this that's gone on, I'll have to release you, it's time anyway, you've been in for four years, no one will question my releasing you." "No!" She said, "you can't, people will know, I was foolish to come here, but don't make it worse, don't release me unless you release everybody else." "I can't do that Rachel, I can't have an adulteress woman as a leader in the ward!" "I'm not an adulteress woman!" She yelled! "It was only that night, only that once!" "Look," he said. "I can't Rachel, I can't, you won't have the guidance of the spirit with this on your conscience ! I have to release you! I may have to excommunicate you as well! People are dead, this is serious!" He said. "No Bishop, you can't, you can't, not now you can't, later, but not now, I'll get a lawyer involved Bishop, I will, you're defaming me, you can't do this!" The threat of a lawyer gave him pause, he had heard of this before, defamation law suits, he had been warned to avoid such situations.

He thought about it and said, "I'll give you some time Rachel, in the interim, pass your responsibilities on to your counselors, avoid contact with other members, tell them your sick, which you are, spiritually sick! I won't say a word, but you need to get this cleaned up, cleaned up with yourself, your family, with the law in Cedar City. Ultimately it's your decision whether you repent or not, Christ atonement will heal this but you must confess your sins to receive forgiveness! Until you confess to your husband, you can't be forgiven! Adultery violates God's commandments, but your sin is also against your husband, your family, you've betrayed them, cheated on them Rachel, this is adultery, don't fool yourself, you have violated your sacred oath of marriage to your husband, to your family, you have to confess to them! Ask your husband to forgive you and he will! As a Christian he is required to forgive you!" She interrupted, "he won't Bishop, I know my own husband, he won't. He will divorce me and take my daughter. If it were just me, I wouldn't care, but I can't do that, not now, not to my daughter. You've seen what happens to kids in this ward, I can't do that to her, not now." "I understand" he said, "but you can't drag this out forever, you'll descend into hell, become a, a soulless raving banshee! Your spirit, screaming out alone, in silence, this is what Hell is! This is what Hell is! Living in sin, knowing what you've done, knowing it's consequences to others! Those people died, this is serious, you must repent," insisted the Bishop. "When my daughter is grown and she has her own family, then Bishop, I will repent, after I know she can survive this, then I will tell her, tell him, but not until then. I know my daughter can't survive it now, she cant, and I cant bear the thought of what will become of her if she knows. I cant! This is the only way, the only way."

The Bishop looked at her intently and said, "your daughter won't survive her mother becoming an empty hollow shell of her former self. You won't survive! That's not going to work," he said.   The Bishop looked down and thought for a moment then quoted a scripture, "do not delay the day of your repentance." She looked at him, shook her head, "this is impossible, there is no way out, I can't do this anymore, I can't, she said, I'm exhausted, this was a mistake, I've got to get away, somehow get away, somewhere, anywhere, just get away."

He said to her as she went to the door, "you can't run from yourself Rachel. She turned to him with a look of disbelief and bewilderment, as if he could not understand the impossible situation she was in.

For the first time in her life, all that she had been taught about the saving Grace of Christ was before her now, but she had never taken it to heart, never accepted it into her soul. Her artificial life was spinning out of control and out of her fear, she rejected the forgiveness and healing of her God. She walked out of the Bishops office without saying another word. Leaving the church, furious, frustrated and determined to keep her silence. As she walked out of the building she heard the congregation break into song, the words she knew all too well, "Choose the right, when a choice is placed before you." The words haunted her now, she had known them, sung them, since she was a child, but now, the impact of that song hit her like never before. The consequences of failing to choose the right, the awful consequences, now filled and dominated her entire world.

From this defiant unrepentant moment forward, her life would be a lie, she would be on stage, pretending to be what she used to be, playing the part others required of her, because of her, there was no part left. She was dead inside. She would act the part of a mother, act the part of a wife, acting for her daughter, but for herself she only knew an unforgiven silent hell, a prison of guilt, anguish and remorse. She knew her selfish act of adultery, indirectly caused the deaths of two wonderful people, and harmed many others, who loved and counted on those people. She knew that it also threatened the only person in this world that she truly loved, her daughter. She feared that her punishment for sin would be the loss of her daughter. She feared that if she confessed, her husband would take her daughter and leave, and of that, he very well might. Her path to forgiveness blocked, by the fear of losing the only person she clung to in life, her only child, her daughter.

She left the church that day alone, angry, bitter and unrepentant, rejecting what she needed most, the forgiving Grace of Christ. She left the community that believed in the ancient standards, the standards that put love above materialism, love above pride and selfish satisfaction. She left those with the courage to confess their sins. Those who dedicate themselves to forgive each other, to love one another, and strive to live the standards of their God.

In her greatest sin, her sin of pride, she rejected that community, her community, and became one of the countless, isolated, ravenous hoards who choose to rage inside the solitary confinement of their own self imposed prison. Those who are driven by fear, people who put pride and arrogance above all else, who put wealth above love, status above substance, image above reality, heart and character. She became one of the innumerable souls who reject the ancient wisdom and choose to live artificial, plastic, "lives of quiet desperation" without love or any form of sincerity, inside the terror of their own private hell.

"And because iniquity shall abound, the love of many shall wax cold." -Matthew 12:24

The End

Made in the USA
Columbia, SC
05 December 2022